"If I had not come… Oh, Betsy…"
He did not need to paint the picture
any more clearly.

Betsy closed her eyes as she again smelled
the liquor and felt the man's arms about her.
Shuddering, she forced away the image to focus
on her reasons for going to the mission.

Sucking in a deep breath, Betsy faced Edward. If
ever there was an awkward moment, this was it.
Hardly the impression she'd hoped to leave on
Edward when he returned to England and she
met him for the first time again after so many
years. "I know, and I am sorry. I did not use good
judgment, I'll allow that."

"So what possessed you to do such a noddy-cock
thing?"

Betsy felt her anger rise again, but forced herself
to civility. After all, he did have a point. Several,
really. "Everyone else in the house had plans. I
remembered, too late, an appointment at the
mission."

"Surely, someone could have accompanied you."
Edward's tone softened. "Betsy, you are much too
lovely a woman to be unescorted even in safer
areas of London. But down here?"

Betsy flushed with humiliation and pleasure.
Edward thought her lovely? Oh, my!

Books by Carolyn R. Scheidies

Love Inspired Heartsong Presents

A Proper Guardian
The Earl's Ward
The Lady's Hero

CAROLYN R. SCHEIDIES

Carolyn's publishing credits include over two dozen books, both fiction and nonfiction, several of which have garnered awards. She's written for a variety of publications, has a regular newspaper column and has worked as an editor, speaker/teacher and book reviewer. Scheidies lectured at the University of Nebraska at Kearney for several years. She speaks to different groups, leads workshops and now teaches adult enrichment writing classes at Central Community College. Key to her writing is hope. She wants her writing to draw others to know the love and hope that only Jesus Christ can provide.

CAROLYN R. SCHEIDIES

The Lady's Hero

HEARTSONG
PRESENTS

PLEASE RECYCLE
THIS PRODUCT IS RECYCLABLE

Recycling programs
for this product may
not exist in your area.

™ LOVE INSPIRED BOOKS

ISBN-13: 978-0-373-48684-7

THE LADY'S HERO

www.Harlequin.com

Printed in U.S.A.

Trust in the Lord with all thine heart; and lean not unto thine own understanding. In all thy ways acknowledge him, and he shall direct thy paths.
—*Proverbs* 3:5–6

Chapter 1

1805

Edward Denning tugged at the stiff collar that poked his neck uncomfortably. His mother insisted he dress in the mode, though he refused to have neckpoints so high he wouldn't be able to turn his head. Nevertheless, his sister, Angella, declared that in his new turn out he was a regular nob.

He wasn't sure where she picked up the cant phrases she relished using to the chagrin of their lady mother. He merely shook his head and tweaked a curl that escaped her hairpiece.

Again he tugged at the collar. Sensing his mother's gaze, he pulled down his hand and sent her a grimace. She gave him a knowing look. He sighed. He knew that look and straightened. He never did well in very formal occasions. He wondered how often he'd even wear his jacket and breeches after tonight. Yet this night was in his honor.

He was thankful, but could not help wishing for his home in Little Cambrage with his vicar father, Reverend Denning, and his lady mother. He'd been gone so many years studying for the ministry. Now that he'd completed his studies and made his father and mother proud, he would love to spend some time reading and relaxing under the tall trees in the back garden.

There would not be much time at home, and that pained him. The past couple of years, he'd been in contact with William Carey, one of the first missionaries to India, and had begun the transition to the mission field.

While many of his friends who were going into the Church of England drew back in horror that he would even consider associating with dissenters of the Baptist stamp, others, such as his parents and his mentor in London, Reverend Jeremiah, understood and embraced his call to India.

From the time he was in leading strings, following his father on rounds of visitation with his parishioners, he desired to become a vicar like his father. Reverend Denning's was not a faith left at the church on Sunday mornings. No matter what the problem, no matter who needed help, Reverend Denning would do what he could.

That the Earl of Lucashire offered to hold a reception for Edward after his commissioning service was beyond anything he or his parents expected. The earl had always favored his father. In fact, it was only after the fact that Edward learned the earl had been his benefactor, paying his way through school. He never wondered where the finances came from. He should have, considering his father's small stipend and how generous he was with what he had.

Edward was humbled that the earl would support his choice to go to India instead of becoming a vicar in one of the earl's own livings, though the nobleman made it abundantly clear that option was always open.

The reception at Lucashire Hall was everything a young man could have wanted. His little sister, Angella's, eyes widened at the starched-up, uniformed servants and the array of delicacies available to the guests. Her hand clung to his and he was glad for the contact. Nerves unsettled his insides and he hoped he would not disgrace himself or his parents during the evening. After all, he knew only a small number of the guests. Others, he guessed were friends of the earl or his own parents. He smiled and shook hands and listened to inane comments.

After the first rush of congratulations and after most guests had drifted into private groups to talk, Angella approached him. "Come, Edward." Angella, always the hoyden, tugged on his arm. "There is someone I wish you to meet."

He laughed and allowed her to pull him away from a dull conversation between peers who liked to hear their own opinions spoken far too much. "All right. All right." He followed her to a young woman about her age who seemed to be doing little but standing alone by the hearth. "Whoa, Angella. I'm not here to entertain one of your little friends," he said quietly so the young woman would not overhear.

"Oh, Edward." Angella all but stamped her foot.

"You must meet her. You will like her, I promise." What could he do since the young woman, tall for her age, turned her gaze on them?

While dressed in the mode, she moved with a nervous awkwardness that made Edward want to stop her movements. But when she turned her brown eyes on him, he gulped. There was something so deep and compassionate in those eyes that he felt himself drowning. He scarcely heard his sister's introductions and stumbled as he took her hand. "Miss…Miss."

"Miss Elizabeth Carrington, Betsy," supplied his smug sister.

"Ah, Miss Carrington. Pleased." He had learned to do the pretty while in London and knew how to behave in polite society. What he didn't understand was the reason Angella was so intent on the introduction.

"Betsy, my brother, Edward Denning."

The young woman's soft, hesitant tone drew out his protective instincts. "Congratulations. It must be terribly exciting knowing you will soon be sharing the message of Christ with those who live in darkness and have never heard His message of love and hope."

Her understanding took him by surprise. Edward forgot she was still in the schoolroom, forgot he should be circulating among those invited on his account, forgot women weren't supposed to be interested in what he would be doing. Instead, he found himself sitting with his sister and a very attentive young woman whose questions showed she knew and cared what he was about. Later, he found it incredible that he'd spent so much time with the brown-eyed young woman. When his mother found him and reminded him of his obligations, he left Betsy's side with reluctance. Her soft voice stayed with him as she promised to keep him in her prayers.

Miss Elizabeth Carrington watched Edward follow his mother with a sense of both excitement and disquiet. There was so much she wanted to say to him and so much she could not, would not say. In the short time they were together, her heart beat for him. He treated her with a respect and dignity she had not expected from a grown man of a chit still in the schoolroom and not yet presented. If only she were older. If only she weren't so awkward.

Angella confronted her. "Isn't my brother a swell?"

Betsy laughed, covering her mouth with her gloved hand. "That may be doing it up a bit brown." She paused. "But he is indeed a fine figure of a man."

Angella all but danced on her dainty feet. "And he likes you almost as much as you like him."

Color rose in Betsy's cheeks. She hoped no one overheard the comment. "Shh." Her friend was much too inclined to state her opinion for all the world to hear.

Angella lowered her voice. "Well, it is true. I wish he was not going so far away."

Silently Betsy agreed, and yet his willingness to follow what he believed to be God's direction was one of the very things that drew her to him.

She blushed again when Angella whispered, "He's better than his picture, isn't he?"

Betsy watched Edward interacting with the peers and others at the reception with such ease. "Oh yes, much better." Her thoughts spun back to her introduction to the man who didn't even know he'd captured her heart. It was two years earlier and she had been a mere thirteen at the time. It happened at a special birthday celebration for the earl's only son, her cousin Spensor, who was like a brother to her.

As long as Betsy had the protection of her cousin, she enjoyed the food and games. Eventually, he had guests to meet and greet and she was once more left on her own. As she made her way toward her mother, who was on the other side of the lawn talking to a woman who emphasized her words with elaborate hand movements, the young viscount who earlier had challenged her to a horse race and which she'd won handily, fell into step beside her.

"Why are you here?" she asked, nervous at his nearness.

"I fear I took losing the race rather poorly." He flicked away a tiny winged creature that had the audacity to land on his fine, tailored jacket.

Betsy stopped and glanced over at him. "Don't tell me you came to apologize for your singular lack of manners."

"Not exactly." He dipped his head as though in acknowledgment of his behavior, and Betsy actually felt her hopes rise.

"Then what?"

"A rematch. Only I get to ride that prime piece of cattle this time." He hesitated.

Betsy pulled her shawl more closely around her shoulders as she felt the cool of the late afternoon breeze on her skin. "I do not think that wise."

A leer twisted his otherwise pleasant features. "As I thought. Without the stallion, you have nothing—*are*

Not long thereafter Reverend Denning helped Betsy and Angella from the gig. "Now, girls, we won't be long, but there is something I want to check before we return with your mother's basket."

Angella led Betsy into the small but cozy home. Betsy was surprised by the taste with which it had been decorated. "Why, this is very nice." She caught the wry grin on Angella's face and blushed. "I've never been in a place like this before."

With that, Angella showed Betsy around the house, not that there was much to see. As they returned to the small drawing room, Betsy stopped before the family painting over the fireplace mantel. The face of the young man in the painting caught her attention. His deep blue eyes seemed to look right into her heart. "You…you have a brother?"

Angella nodded and stared up at the painting. "It's not a masterpiece like the paintings at Lucashire Hall, but the itinerant painter did a credible job. Finished, oh, about six months ago."

Betsy brought her attention back to the young man. "Your brother…" She had to know more.

"Yes, my friend, my protector, my big brother." No doubt Angella was proud of him.

"He wasn't at Lucashire."

"No, Edward is off training to be a minister of the gospel. He has always wanted to help others. Very like Father, he is."

Betsy could scarcely breathe. "Edward. It is a strong name, that. He has deep, wise, kind eyes." She did not know what else to say. All she knew was that she could not get enough of the stories Angella was more than willing to tell about her brother, and she never ever forgot the picture on the mantel of that humble vicarage. It was then Betsy began to pray for the man in the picture.

Some weeks after Edward's reception, Betsy found herself in London with her parents. She hadn't been so sure about the trip to London. Her father had his government responsibilities, which he took very seriously. Her mother insisted they go with him and enjoy the activities and shopping London provided. While Betsy found the theater exciting and the architecture fascinating, she was thrilled when her father suggested a ride in the park.

Betsy always did better on the back of a horse than on her feet, which had trouble going the same direction at the same time or not stumbling over the least little thing. Her smile was one of pure pleasure as she reined the horse through the entrance to the park late that same afternoon.

Large trees shielded the park proper from the noise of the outside world. The chestnut tossed his head and tried to grab for the bit. With a laugh, Betsy kept control of the animal, enjoying the struggle for mastery. Her new habit fit her maturing figure, though Betsy wondered if she'd ever fill out or would always be tall and gangly. She sighed. Her mind flitted to Edward. Since the reception she'd thought of him often. She blushed. She'd even dreamed about him. She wished she lived closer to his sister to ask when he was to leave for India or if he had already left.

When her father indicated a direction, Betsy nodded and followed. She sat tall on the sixteen-hand gelding. She winced—a tall young woman on a tall horse. Not exactly geared to bring out the suitors. Not that she was in the market—not yet at any rate. That would come in a few years. As her thoughts turned once more to Edward, she spied several young men ambling along, talking, laughing and, from the looks of their gestures, having a lively discussion.

When one young man took off his hat, Betsy started. That blond hair looked familiar. The man riffled his hair, gestured and stuck the hat back onto his head. Edward? Could Edward possibly be here now? Obviously the man was with friends or colleagues and very focused on their discussion.

Betsy's throat tightened. She had to know. The more she watched him, the more she was convinced that the man was indeed Edward. Oh my. The dictates of society kept her from hailing him when she rode by on the chestnut gelding. She slowed enough to get a better look, but the animal was less than cooperative. She also must not lose sight of her father ahead of her. Oh, bother!

Nonetheless, as she rode by, Edward stopped dead, seemingly forgetting his companions as he watched her handle the large, rambunctious animal.

For a moment, Betsy wondered if he judged her, knowing, as did she, it was not the thing for a lady to ride anything but a docile horse in the park where the ton took leisurely turns about the walkways or drove about in carriages to see and be seen. As good a horsewoman as she was, with all the people about, she held the rambunctious animal to a walk with some difficulty.

The afternoon was overcast, but warm enough to require only a light cape. She wore a Devonshire brown habit with gold braid trim and a hat set at a rakish angle. Betsy knew herself to be awkward on foot, but also was woman enough to recognize she was all that was grace and elegance on the back of the horse that she forced to a quick-paced walk.

She glanced over at the man she thought to be Edward, hoping he'd see her at her best. She recalled his passion as he told her about his call to India. She recalled, too, his handsome features, caring smile and captivating blue eyes. She heard his deep voice speaking with such fervor. Her pulse quickened at the thought of speaking with him again.

She shook her head. Was she daft? Why would he even remember his conversation with a young, insignificant woman when he had such a grand call on his life and was about to sail away to the grandest adventure and challenge ever? Mayhap she mistook someone who looked like Edward for him. Riding with her father beside her, she did not have the courage to turn back. Still, she was about to suggest that very thing to her father when they came upon an open carriage and her father stopped to speak to the occupants, who turned out to be her mother and a couple of her friends.

Betsy tried to hold her horse still, but he continued to fidget and tug at the bit. She circled him about and glanced back. The man she thought was Edward seemed to be heading her direction. For a moment, she held her breath.

His companions seemed less than eager to follow. He stopped.

Betsy willed him to continue, wished for the freedom and the courage to go to him without finding herself beyond the pale of strict London societal dictates. *Oh, Lord, why taunt me with him?*

She could not help staring at him. Was the blond, well-proportioned man the one who made her heart beat faster? When he glanced toward her, she saw him more clearly. Surely it was indeed Edward, wasn't it? Silently they exchanged a smile.

He started toward her at the very moment Betsy's father called to her. All she could do was send the man a nod of acknowledgment and follow her father and her mother's carriage out of the park and out of his life.

Edward watched Betsy ride out of his life, and his heart sank within him. She was a superb rider. He would have loved riding alongside her. It was not to be. Again circumstances parted them. He sighed. It was just as well. He had no time for courtship or marriage or anything else. And she was so young. It would be years before he could court her anyway, even if it were possible.

He chided himself for so easily losing focus on his dream, his calling, his mission. His friends joined him. "She's quite the thing."

"Who is she?"

Their interest somehow tainted the encounter, and Edward quickly directed their attention back to their discussion about matters of faith and politics. Later that evening, he savored the chance encounter, wondering if indeed it was chance at all. Still and all, he had little time to spend daydreaming about what would never be.

Every waking moment, he prepared for the voyage into the unknown. Reverend Jeremiah assisted him in so many ways, making the transition much easier by advising him about what to pack, how much and what to take and making the proper connections for travel. The next month, he shipped out to India. He left his sister in the capable hands of his parents and tried to forget Betsy altogether. It didn't work.

Chapter 2

1810

Edward's work in India taxed him mentally, physically and spiritually. Had it been years since he arrived? It felt like months, and it felt like an eternity. He was bone weary and glad to return home after a long trip into the interior. He groaned when his man handed him several pieces of mail. "For you."

For the moment, Edward let them sit on the side table. He was exhausted and not sure whether he was more elated with the slight success he and his fellow missionary had with sharing the gospel of Christ or disheartened by the darkness practiced by so many. He did know he was dirty and sweaty and was more than ready for the bath drawn for him.

Later, as he pulled on one of the jackets he'd brought

with him from England, he realized he'd lost weight, but gained strength. Though leaner, his body was more used to physical exercise than the son of a beloved vicar or the ministerial student in London. Regular horseback riding and walking had never shaped him like the rigors of being in the field.

Edward riffled a hand through his blond hair. In the reflection of the silver teapot, he could see his hair had returned to its normal light color from the gray-brown from weeks of dust stirred up by miles and miles of travel on dirt-packed roads. Leaning back in his cushioned and well-used chair, Edward closed his eyes, just for a moment, as he awaited the meal, the odors of which already teased his taste buds.

It had been a lonely few years, though satisfying in many ways. He knew he had been right to follow William Carey to India and to heed God's call on his life. The people needed so much, needed God's love most of all. Love. It was the reason he was willing to give up his dreams of becoming a vicar like his father.

But he had given up more. His dreams often teased with images of a wife and family. How he yearned for a woman to love and to be loved in return. Had he really believed those desires would fade with time? How foolish. "Oh, God," he whispered, not for the first or the hundredth time, "if this is not to be, please take away this desire."

Instead, as he relaxed he recalled a young woman with intense brown eyes. He sucked in a breath, surprised the memory was as sharp as though it had happened yesterday. Though he tried, he'd never forgotten her. There were times he was almost sure he felt her prayers. But that was fanciful thinking.

By now, she would have forgotten all about the missionary she had met one night, what was it, four years ago? By now she might well have the bronze of a season and a husband. By now he should have been able to let his image of her go. Miss Betsy Carrington's image always came to mind whenever he thought of love and marriage. How foolish, and yet... He shook his head at his useless fancies. Time to let all that go.

After a meal that warmed his insides, Edward sorted through the mail. One from the Reverend Avery Jeremiah in London. The minister had been a younger son of a peer who, with an independent portion, entered the church, not because he had to, but because he felt a genuine calling on his life. Edward smiled. The man had become both mentor and friend as well as a solid supporter of his missionary endeavor. Another post came from a supporting church. The last one caught his attention. From Angella? Odd the letter wasn't marked from his father. A frown touched his lips as he unfolded the parchment and read...

Dear Edward,
It is my grievous duty to inform you of the death
of both Mother and Father.

In her neat flowing handwriting, Angella explained the circumstances surrounding the deaths of first their father, then their mother of illness.

As I am alone now with no idea of how to go on,
I pray you will see your way clear to return home
at least for a time.
    I shall write Grandfather to acquaint him with

the passing on of his daughter. I will tell him, also, of my need, but I sincerely doubt he will heed my letter any more than he heeded letters Mother wrote since her marriage to Father.

Wherever I go, I will try to leave word here at the vicarage so you can find my direction and come to me directly.

I am sorry to be the one to give you this news, but, as you know, there is no one else.

If you're wondering about Mrs. Adams, who so faithfully looked after us since we were children in leading strings, she passed on some six months past.

Please come home, Edward.
Ever, your sister,
Angella

The letter fluttered to the floor as Edward buried his head in his hands. "Oh, Lord, no! No!" His dear parents were gone. And his little sister was without home or protector. How could that be? Obviously, she had not had a season. Mayhap no funds for one. Father was a bit too generous with his meager stipend.

He reached to pick up the letter and checked the date. She had sent it months ago. Pulling on his boots, Edward scrambled to his feet. He had to go home. He had to go now! He had to book passage, but how? His finances were marginal at best. It mattered not. Angella needed him. Somehow he would find a way home. Sitting down he wrote her a letter he hoped would arrive before he did.

Glancing around, Edward decided the ship wasn't much. The crew bustled about him, ignoring him for the most part as long as he kept out of the way. More than once Edward found himself bumped or accidentally pushed as sailors rushed to trim sails or otherwise make adjustments.

Until he came on board, he had not realized how tired he felt, how often he forgot to eat or care for his own needs. Had not realized the difference until he packed up his clothes—worn and probably far out of fashion—and dressed in clothes that had once snugly fit his figure. His clothes now hung on a frame that had grown lean. He grimaced as he looked down his length. His old acquaintances would probably think of him as quite the quiz these days—if they recognized him at all. Yes. He had become odd far away from England and the pleasure-seeking haunts of London, odd and very much alone.

Edward sucked in a breath. As much as he tried to let the desire go, he wanted a helpmate. He desired a woman who would love him, care for him and be at his side no matter what. He grimaced. Unlikely. What had he to offer the sort of woman he'd want to make his wife? Exactly nothing.

He shuddered thinking about the young women who sailed out to India when they didn't "take" after a season or two or three in London. These young women, termed "the fishing fleet," and their parents figured that with the prevalence of the military in the country and few English women to choose from, the young women would be better able to find husbands.

Any Englishman was ripe for the plucking. Those desperate young women were one reason he tried to stay away from the government compounds and invitations to parties, balls and dinners. He almost felt sorry for families who hoped to increase their consequence or finances by trapping some unsuspecting soldier into marriage.

Not all women were of that stamp. Edward's thoughts drifted back to the brown eyes that so captivated him—Miss Betsy Carrington's eyes. No matter what, he was unable to get his chance encounter out of his mind—if it was a chance encounter. He'd come to recognize what seemed like chance often had God's hand in it. He did know that those brown eyes invaded his nights when he least expected them. He felt the draw of wife and family and prayed for release. None came.

He shook his head. For the time being he needed to focus on his sister. Everything cycled back to Angella. Surely she'd found a safe place....

For all his concern for his sister, his heart refused to let go of that image of brown eyes and the woman he'd actually spoken to but once. Betsy. The name always brought a smile. Her image warmed his heart and set his mind on what he tried so valiantly to release—a wife. As the ship sailed onward home to England, he looked up into the sky. "Lord, one way or another I need to know. Please, might I possibly see Betsy Carrington again?"

Miss Elizabeth Carrington, Betsy, was once again in London, this time for the season. Her mother, cousin Spensor—now the Earl of Lucashire—and Lord and Lady Alistair, who opened their London home for the season, were giving her and Angella a London season. So much had happened the past few weeks she could scarcely take it in.

Betsy grabbed Angella's hands and danced around the parlor. "Finally cousin Spensor has seen the light."

Angella's green eyes sparkled as she disengaged herself from Betsy's grasp. "It was quite the night."

Betsy stopped and tugged at her sleeve, which kept riding up her arm. She tucked a strand of her long, dark hair behind her ear and grimaced. Of course, her hair had already started to unravel from the coiffure her maid had fashioned earlier that morning. She'd refused to cut her long locks, so her maid fashioned it up with tendrils dangling teasingly about her cheeks. She was told the style was flattering to her height and long, narrow face as it added some width.

All Betsy knew was that it was also increasingly irritating. Mayhap cutting it would be less frustration, though she'd always felt her dark hair was her one redeeming feature. She tugged on a curl and ended with her hair loose about her shoulders.

Her excitement exerted itself again. "Think about it. I am in transports that, finally, you and cousin Spensor are engaged! I mean, no more trying to get you two together. Oops!" She bit her lip and backed up, only to trip. Angella's quick grab prevented a fall.

"You all right?" Angella asked before releasing her arm.

Betsy rolled her eyes. "I wish I didn't so easily get tangled up in my own feet. A London season and lessons in dancing and decorum haven't done much to change that." She sighed and drew Angella down on the sofa beside her. "But now that you are engaged to the Earl of Lucashire—" she straightened and posed with dignity "—the rest of the season will be fun for you. Though it will probably continue to be a trial for me."

"Perhaps not," Angella encouraged. "You may yet find a suitor. The season is not over by any means."

Angella's soft spring-green gown complemented Betsy's sky-blue gown. Angella gazed at the ring Spensor had given her just that morning. "Oh, Betsy," she said, changing the topic, "how could I have ever imagined that the Earl of Lucashire and I would have a future together? When my parents died so unexpectedly, I thought my life was over. And yet something wonderful has come out of tragedy." Tears filled her eyes and Betsy squeezed her hand.

"My dearest cousin has been caught right and tight and I could not be more pleased. Oh, Angella, Spensor was always like a big brother to me. We'll almost be sisters as well as bosom bows. I only hope…"

This time Angella smiled and squeezed her hands. "You hope for a similar outcome."

Betsy could not entirely keep her face from showing what she wished to hide from her best friend.

Angella frowned. "Betsy, you do want to get married, don't you? Isn't that why they parade us all over London for the season? I know it was different for me. After all, I already…"

"I know, had a *tendre* for my cousin. Now we get to plan your official engagement party." Betsy sighed a happy, dreamy sigh. "Then we plan the wedding."

"Not so fast, Betsy. First, we plan your coming-out ball."

"*La,* and I'll trip over my feet, rip my gown and make a cake of myself."

"Not by half. Spensor will see to that…unless you have developed a partiality for another eligible *parti* and prefer another escort."

Angella's gaze narrowed at Betsy's blush. "So you *have* formed a partiality. But I have seen you do little but call the young dandies flocking around us by such positive names as mutton-headed, addlepated and taken with their own consequence. So who is the paragon for whom you pine? One of the young men who've taken us walking in the park or done the pretty for us at the theater, ball or other events we seem to always be attending?" She rolled her eyes.

Betsy started to rise, but Angella tugged her back down. "Surely the young man isn't some fribble, fop or scapegrace."

Betsy shook her head. "No…no, never. Really, Angella you refine too much from my expression."

"I do not think so." Betsy all but wilted under her friend's all too discerning gaze and struggled for a way to again distract her attention. Without thinking, she blurted, "Remember when we first met?"

"Very much so." Angella's gaze held a faraway look. "Yes. I scarcely knew how to go on. The birthday party Spensor's father, the old, beloved earl, threw for him with the assistance of your mother, was quite the thing. Overwhelming really."

"Don't I know it? I was all of thirteen. Even then the young people my age found it more entertaining to bait and put me down for my gracelessness…."

"Except on the back of a horse."

"Of course," Betsy agreed. "Which was part of the problem that day." She remembered all too well the hurt she had felt that day and her surprise when a girl she'd never seen interceded, acting as her long-lost friend. "What you did that day took courage, Angella. I was so glad to get away for a while when you asked me to

accompany you and your father back to the vicarage."
Remembering the rest, Betsy knew she'd led herself
right down the wrong path. She lowered her head so
Angella would not detect the pink in her cheeks. She
should have known better.

"I remember how you gazed at our family portrait."
A teasing grin lifted Angella's lips. "At least you kept
gazing at *one* member of the family and asking lots of
questions about my handsome, if I do say so myself,
older brother."

"Argh!" Betsy's hands covered her flaming cheeks.
"Please, Angella."

Angella stopped immediately, her tone kind. "It has
always been my brother, Edward, hasn't it?"

Betsy closed her eyes for a moment. "I know he's
on his way back from India. Do you think…" She let
the words trail.

"That Edward might arrive in time for my wedding?"

Betsy gulped. She might as well be truthful. "For
my coming-out."

A soft expression darkened Angella's eyes. "I hope
so. I certainly hope so. But I am not sure where he is
at present or when he'll arrive. He doesn't know about
me or Spensor or anything but that our folks are gone. I
wrote him that I had no place to go, which I didn't have
at the time." Angella caught Betsy's hand.

"I don't want you to pine for Edward. This is your
season. Give some of those young bucks a chance to
steal your heart, at least a chance."

"We'll see," Betsy told her. "All I want is for a fairy-
tale ending like you have."

"But without all the nightmares in between."

"True," Betsy agreed.

"Enough of this." Angella got up and pulled Betsy up beside her. "We have a coming-out party to plan."

"And an engagement party."

Together they chorused, "And a wedding to plan."

The two girls grinned at each other, as Betsy added, "All that and more. Come on. Let's find my mother and Lady Alistair and begin planning."

Angella rolled her eyes. "If Lady Alistair and Lady Carrington haven't already gotten together to plan it all for us."

Betsy laughed ruefully, well aware of how her mother, Lady Carrington, and Winter, Lady Alistair, were enjoying the season launching the two young women.

Betsy watched Angella stand, turn and turn again as the dressmaker poked, tucked, nodded and grumbled as she fitted the gown to her friend's petite figure.

Angella nodded, but her expression showed the strain of an afternoon of shopping for material, fripperies and accessories that Lady Carrington and Lady Alistair declared were absolutely necessary for the bride-to-be. They'd returned home only to have the dressmaker show up with a host of underlings to turn ideas into confections of perfection for Betsy's coming-out and Angella's engagement parties as well as the host of other events to which they had been invited. The girls exchanged a glance of perfect understanding.

Betsy rolled her eyes, as tired of this round as Angella. Her response caused Angella to swallow a giggle with a forced cough. "I do think it high time you get fitted now, Betsy." Angella touched the dressmaker's shoulder to garner her attention. "I need a rest. Are you not almost finished for now?"

The dressmaker muttered something in French too low and quick for Betsy to comprehend, but she guessed the phrase was not something she intended innocent young women to hear. The woman, an émigré from France, was one of many who came to England to escape Napoleon's domination. Like many others, she had stayed even after he was safely deposed.

A moment later, she switched to accented but clear English. "Yes. I have take the measurements. This will do." She moved back, allowing Angella to step off the stool on which she'd been standing. Too long it appeared, as Angella tottered when she tried to step down. Betsy reached out a hand to steady her and almost brought them both to the floor. "Oh, Angella, I am sooo sorry. I only meant to help." Her cheeks burned with mortification.

Recovering quickly, Angella shook her head. "No, Betsy. It was my fault. I didn't realize my leg had gone to sleep." Angella rubbed her thigh as she grimaced. "Let it go, Betsy. We're both right and tight." Angella pushed Betsy toward the dressmaker's stool. "Go on. I'll rest and let you do the pretty for Madame Dubois for a while."

Betsy merely nodded, thankful her friend understood. She also understood Angella was not about to let her take full responsibility for the incident. Nonetheless, Betsy bit her lip, frustrated that, once more, her gracelessness caused a problem. Only this time it didn't just affect her.

She could imagine Angella with a broken leg, hobbling down the aisle on her wedding day. That wouldn't do, wouldn't do by half. She could see her cousin determinedly carrying his bride-to-be up the aisle, and that brought a smile. Still, she did not wish to cause more problems for the two, who had already been through so much.

A small voice inside told her, *But Angella did not fall. You did not fall. Mayhap you dwell much too much on all this.* Did she? She had always been told by her peers, in graphic detail as they laughed, pointed and made fun, just how awkward and clumsy they considered her to be. Not that she needed witnesses to her gracelessness. Betsy sent her prayer heavenward. *Am I truly not the antidote I have always believed myself to be?*

Though she heard no voice, a peace settled deep inside. Mayhap, just mayhap, there was hope for her. With that heady thought, Betsy stepped onto the stool. Betsy turned, lifted an arm, put an arm down and tried not to tumble off the stool as the dressmaker adjusted, pinned and clipped. Up and down, on and off the stool, Betsy followed directions as the dressmaker worked with several different gowns and patterns for jackets and capes. Twice she stumbled but caught herself.

The dressmaker muttered under her breath as she worked and seemed a whole lot less enthusiastic about her fittings than those of Angella. But then, she was tall with not much of a figure, while Angella was petite but nicely curvaceous. Betsy sighed and shoved down the jealousy that threatened to rise.

Betsy's exhaustion and boredom faded as Madame

Dubois began fitting her for her coming-out gown. It came together as she moved at the dressmaker's terse directions. "It will be so beautiful," she all but breathed to the delight of the dressmaker, who even managed a smile and nod.

Angella surveyed her in the pieced-together creation. "You'll be bang up to the mark in that gown." Getting to her feet, she acted out the scenario. "Why, you will leave them all dropping their quizzing glasses." Even the dressmaker managed a thin smile.

The dressmaker straightened shoulders usually bowed with her labors. The woman should be proud. Betsy could not wait to see the completed creation. The gown consisted of a sleeveless shell of muted peach with a fine lace overlay, which filled in the scooped neckline with lace and added lacy sleeves that finished with a ruffle at the wrists. The whole would be a gown Betsy would not soon forget. Excitement rose. In this gown, even she would look stunning.

Angella agreed. "Truly, Betsy, it is a lovely gown for you."

A maid brought in a tray at that moment and Angella sat down. As Betsy continued to follow directions, her friend popped a large strawberry dipped in chocolate into her mouth.

Moments later, her stomach growled embarrassingly loud as she watched Angella, who sat on a rich brown-textured settee eating miniature sandwiches and slices of fruit purchased fresh that morning and drinking lemonade. With a decided sparkle of mischief in her eyes, Angella exaggerated her enjoyment of the repast. "Delicious. Want a strawberry? How about this?" She held up a sweetmeat she then popped into her mouth. Then she giggled.

Betsy wrinkled her nose at her friend. She was so distracted she all but fell off the stood. The dressmaker grabbed her arms, just in time, much to Betsy's mortification.

Chapter 3

The next day found Betsy, Angella and Lady Carrington far away from London's glitz, glamour and high society. Angella sat beside Lucashire, who handled with a deft hand the matched black horses pulling the carriage. Behind them in the second seat of the well-sprung carriage sat Betsy and her mother. A tiger, perched in back, waited to take the horses when Spensor and the ladies entered the small mission in a part of town few ladies ever visited.

This day, they passed out clothing for a host of young children whose parents scarcely kept body and soul together. Most worked jobs that demanded long hours for little pay.

It broke Betsy's heart to see the delight of the children when they received a new outfit or two and to watch parents who struggled between wounded pride at needing the assistance and the excitement of their children. It embarrassed Betsy to think the lovely clothing from the children of her mother's friends had been cast off after being worn but once or twice. Still and all, she sent up a prayer of thanks the parents passed the clothing on to her mother instead of simply discarding them.

Her mother knew how to treat the parents with a dignity that, at least somewhat, eased their tension. Afterward, Betsy, Angella, Lady Carrington and Lucashire stayed to listen to a short, wide preacher who spoke the Word true enough, but who also made it so dry Betsy had difficulty staying awake. Still, those from the neighborhood listened, slightly forward, as though searching for something. Searching for hope? Betsy knew they hungered for God and prayed. Her mother told her those who supported the concept of the mission, such as the Reverend Avery Jeremiah, a minister of some note, ensured that someone—often ministerial students or missionaries back from the field—filled the pulpit as needed.

Betsy always felt a bit depressed after visiting the mission. Lady Winter pulled her out of it by suggesting the ladies ride in the park the next morning. Lady Carrington begged off. Her excuses did not surprise Betsy. Her heavyset mother never did understand her daughter's fascination with riding, though, like her deceased father, her mother took pride that their daughter cut quite a dash on horseback.

The next day when they mounted their horses, which were held by grooms looking smart in Alistair livery, Betsy glanced around. She waited until both Winter and

Angella gathered their reins. It appeared they were riding alone except for a lone groom on a tall bay.

Winter caught Betsy's look of speculation. "It is all right. I am a matron of an age to chaperone two gently bred young ladies."

Angella spoke up. "Everything else is so prescribed in London society, I thought we'd not be allowed out without a male escort."

Besty nudged her mount into a walk. "Any chance we can find a place to test the mettle of these animals?"

Winter laughed. "I understand how you feel, Betsy, truly. While I'll shrug off some of society's stringent dictates, I will not do anything to harm your chances for the season."

Angella grinned. "I'm already taken."

"Betsy is not." Winter led the way. "My job is to show my charges off to advantage. And since we're all horsewomen, we show off well on horseback." She paused. "Besides, I was getting quite resty to get back on a horse. I miss my morning gallops with Alistair at home."

The three remained silent for a time as they negotiated through busy traffic to the relative quiet of the park. They entered under a canopy of trees that Betsy guessed had graced the area for hundreds of years. The hooves of the horses clip-clopped against the hard-packed path. The relative quiet gave way to a clatter of people, horses and vehicles. Women in the latest styles flirted gaily with men in breeches, highly polished boots and fitted jackets.

More than one gentleman acknowledged their presence, and the ladies found themselves scarcely able to move forward at times. Betsy's mare shook her head, while Angella's champed on the bit.

A shy, thin peer in a chocolate-brown coat that matched that of his gelding rode up. Winter introduced him as Baron Fritton. He bowed so low, Betsy stilled a giggle, fearing he'd fall off his prime cattle and giving silent thanks he did not. As he addressed them, his gaze kept gliding toward her. His manner was gentle and Betsy, to her surprise, quite liked him. Before she had time to consider the matter, she found she had agreed to a dance at the ball to which they were promised the next evening.

After he moved on, Winter grinned. "Betsy, I think you made a conquest."

"Oh my. That happened all too quickly." Betsy felt her cheeks grow warm and couldn't even glance toward Angella. What would she think about it all? It mattered not, for at that moment the wheel of the carriage ahead of them on the path snapped and crumbled. While the occupants appeared fine, Betsy's less-than-docile mount was not. In an instant, the mare threw up her head and tried to bolt. It took all of Betsy's considerable skill to settle the mount down. Once she was in control again, she glanced up to find her performance applauded by several gentleman, who knew enough to remain silent during her struggle, but who stayed alert and on the ready to come to the rescue should the need arise.

A broad-shouldered peer raised his hat and nodded. "Magnificent, Miss…"

Winter supplied, "Miss Elizabeth Carrington, the Marquis of Beddinlong."

Betsy did not know how to deal with the man's attention. Her success on horseback was more than what she'd achieved in all her outings so far in London. She did not wish to consider how they would view her when they interacted with her without the horse. Still, she rather enjoyed feeling worthy of such attention.

As they slowly walked their horses through the park, Betsy remembered another ride in a London park. She forgot the gentleman who so recently flattered as her thoughts spun back to the second and last time she'd seen Edward.

It was in London, at this very park. At least, she was almost sure it was him, if her heart hadn't made her see what she only wished to see. She'd thought about that day many times since and still wasn't completely sure. The memory was less than satisfactory. Yet she held it close.

Edward probably never knew she'd actually seen him in the park just before he'd left for India. But where was Edward now?

Though flagging with exhaustion, Edward pushed himself to locate his sister. His first stop was Little Cambrage, where he had grown to manhood. The townspeople sent questioning glances his way as he drove by. He doubted anyone recognized him. As he stopped in front of the vicarage, memories flooded his mind—his mother's smile, his father's gentle strength, Angella's mischievous grin. Swallowing the lump in his throat, Edward jumped to the ground.

Fastening the reins to the post, Edward straightened his shoulders and walked up the path to the door.

From his first glimpse of Reverend Carter sitting behind his large kidney-shaped desk in the paneled study, Edward felt reserve. There was something about the man's eyes, something cold and calculating that gave Edward pause.

Reverend Carter's gaze narrowed when Edward introduced himself. "Sit down, Reverend Denning. You are a reverend, are you not?"

Edward nodded curtly. It seemed strange to be addressed as Reverend Denning here in the vicarage. Edward almost glanced around, expecting to see his father behind him. His heart sank. He'd never again hear his father's footsteps or feel the palpable power of his prayers. It was a deep loss, and the young man felt it keenly.

Before he could ask about Angella, Reverend Carter rang for afternoon tea, tea and nothing more. Edward was forced to mouth polite conversation when he wished to ask after his sister. The delay made him nervous.

He waited until the sullen maidservant briskly removed the tray. "Now, Reverend Carter, I'm sure you understand my concern about my sister. I came here hoping you might give me her direction."

The man's lips tightened. "That I can, though being a man of God as you are, I am certain you will not care to hear the truth of the matter."

Fear ate at Edward, but he let nothing show on his face. "Is she well?"

"In a manner of speaking." Reverend Carter sat forward, obviously relishing his role of informer. "Let me explain that I offered for your sister, but she turned me down."

Edward did not blame his sister for turning down this pompous bore. He did not voice this opinion, but from the look on Carter's face, the vicar understood the direction of his thoughts.

"If you'll provide her direction, I shall be on my way." He put a conciliatory smile on his face.

"She's not in the village, has not been since soon after the passing of your parents. It didn't take her long to throw herself at the Earl of Lucashire."

"The earl is a good man. I don't see—"

"You mean the last earl. His profligate son bears the title now."

As Edward's eyes flashed, Carter hurried on. "She lived with him for some time without benefit of chaperone. The situation was so disgraceful, I understand, the earl's fiancée, Lady Margaret Ainsworth, called off the betrothal when she discovered the true state of affairs."

Edward took this in with a sense of unreality. "I cannot credit it!" He sat back in shock as he stared at the self-satisfied new vicar. "There is some mistake. You don't know my sister."

"Mayhap *you* don't know your sister. How long has it been since you've seen her?"

Edward was hard put to disguise the guilt that flashed across his face.

"As I thought." The vicar leaned back with a smirk on his face that made Edward grit his teeth. "I fear it is true enough. The earl bought off Lady Margaret, or so I heard. He is besotted with your Angella."

Edward relaxed. "Mayhap…"

Reverend Carter shook his head slowly, a pitying smile on his lips. "He certainly did not ask me to perform a wedding." He spread thick hands. "One day she was touted as his ward, the next…who knows?"

Edward sensed there was much left out of the recital the vicar told with such relish. Something was off and yet, yet could there be truth in what the vicar told him? *Please, Lord, no! Let there be some other explanation.*

Edward left the vicarage in shock, hardly noting the baggage the vicar had his man pile into the curricle— all that was left of his father's possessions. He urged on the horses, letting them travel at their own pace as he tried to assimilate Reverend Carter's information.

Surely, surely the vicar was wrong. Edward's head cleared somewhat as he moved slowly through the village. Of course, the vicar wanted her for himself. Someone else would tell him differently.

Drawing up the animals before a small cottage, he went to speak to the woman who truly cared for his mother.

"I fear she was forced to it." This the old woman said sorrowfully. "You see…" She proceeded to explain how the village had turned against the girl and how the earl rescued her. "She was at the earl's mercy. His reputation has not been of the best…a real charmer. I'm sorry, Reverend Denning. Your sister is a dear girl. I'm sure she did not seek to do wrong—mayhap she hasn't." Her lips tightened. "I fear our vicar likes to spin things to his advantage."

Recognizing the woman's sincerity, Edward bowed his head. Pain bore anger, and anger fostered his guilt. There was little left for him in the village. With a heavy heart, the Reverend Edward Denning drove to Lucashire Hall. Though the servant who opened the door looked askance at his disheveled appearance, Edward straightened. "I am Edward Denning, Reverend Denning's son, the former vicar of Little Cambrage." He held in his anxiety with some difficulty.

At this the servant nodded. "Indeed. Good man, the reverend."

"I wish to speak to His Lordship."

"He is not in residence." The expression on the man's face told Edward it was something he should have known since the earl's standard was not flying from the flagpole.

"May I speak to whoever is in charge?"

The servant considered the request. "His Lordship's secretary, Mr. Trowbridge, is here now."

A few minutes later, Edward was shown into a small office, where a man with military bearing sat before a large desk. Ledgers lay open before him. After introductions, Trowbridge offered refreshments Edward was not loath to consume. He tried to use the manners instilled in him from his childhood to eat with decorum and not to stuff the small, fancy sandwiches and sweetmeats into his mouth. He had not eaten since the evening previous. Mr. Trowbridge waited patiently.

With one last swallow and sip of tea, Edward wiped his mouth on the serviette. With a sigh, he turned to the matter at hand. "I stopped to visit with Reverend Carter in Little Cambrage."

"I see." From the frown on Trowbridge's face, Edward surmised the man cared little for the vicar. For some reason that cheered Edward somewhat.

"He sent me here with some tale about Angella…."
Edward hoped Trowbridge would allay his fears.

"With some Banbury tale, I suppose." Trowbridge sighed and moved around papers on his desk as though carefully considering his words. "You realize she is not in residence right now."

"She was here." Edward knew sarcasm bit his words.

"Yes. No thanks to that cravenly vicar." For a moment the man let down his guard. "I shall be in high gig when the man moves on." His gaze held compassion. "Not like your father. Not like him at all."

"I agree." A thin smile touched Edward's lips. "Of my sister. Where is she?"

Trowbridge tented his hands and observed Edward until Edward shifted uncomfortably. He sensed the man read confusion and anger in his expression. "London for the season."

Edward closed his eyes momentarily. "I understand my sister was held here without benefit of chaperone or companion." Anger was definitely gaining sway as he spoke.

Mr. Trowbridge merely surveyed him. "She was well provided for."

"Provided for. Is that what you call using an innocent?" Edward ground out his thoughts about men who do such things.

The secretary was amazingly calm in the face of his outburst. "You are not ready to hear it, but you don't exactly have the right of things. Remember that before you judge too quickly. Still, I imagine you wish their direction."

"I do." Edward gulped back more condemnation, ashamed of his outburst. He managed a weak "I am only concerned for my sister."

"Yes. She'll be happy to have you home." He paused, considering. "Well, I'll tell you what. Write a letter to your sister and I'll send it on to her."

It was the best Edward was able to manage. With ill grace, he composed a letter. Handing it over, he said, "I will be heading toward London."

Nothing Mr. Trowbridge said or didn't say mitigated the reason for Edward's anger. Yet the man had as much as said he wasn't fully in the know. How much worse could the truth be? He left Lucashire Hall angry at the situation, angry at Lucashire and just a bit angry at God. But that he was unwilling to admit.

He thought of all the congregations and donors on his list and sighed. If only the funds weren't needed so badly. If only he could put off his mission until after finding Angella, but no…. Straightening his shoulders, Edward breathed. "Take care of her, Lord. Take care of Angella until I get to her."

For him there was nothing like work to take his mind from all the possibilities. With a vengeance, Edward plunged into his schedule, pushing his animals from place to place on his schedule, always heading in the direction of London. He was moderately successful. If only his heart was not so heavy within him. The sooner he made his contacts, the sooner he'd get to London… and Angella. He began to see himself as a knight on a mission of rescue.

Of what use was his ministry far away in India if he lost those nearest and dearest to him because he had not been here to see to Angella? For all his eloquence, he felt the hypocrite as the rage grew within him. The only thing that cooled his ire were thoughts of the lovely, gentle Betsy Carrington. At times he wondered, to his shame, whether he more desired to get to London to see his sister protected and settled or to run into Miss Betsy Carrington. Now he had returned, but not for Betsy. He must remember why he came—to rescue his sister.

With a long list of stops still to go, the next stop changed everything.

To him it was just one more stop, one more place open for him to speak of the work in India in the opulent parlor of a wealthy donor. As always, he told of Carey's struggle to set up a mission, spoke of his own small congregation. There was no gainsaying the love he held toward the people he had adopted as his own.

As he surveyed the congregation, he was startled by the hostility in the eyes of a tall young woman who watched him intently. Dressed to the nines as she was, there was no doubt she found the whole quite dull. Nonetheless as he mentioned that his father hailed from Little Cambrage, a tight smile formed on her lips—as though she already knew. He had the sense she was simply there to see and be seen and really did not care a fig for his mission. Nonetheless, he'd take what he could. God often moved in mysterious ways.

"Reverend Denning," the woman gushed after the service, "thank you for speaking to us. Of course, my brothers and I will do what we can for those poor unfortunates."

Denning forced a smile. This condescending attitude toward other peoples and cultures always left him in a towering rage he could not show. Why did the English think they had a corner on civilization and intelligence? Nonetheless, he answered politely, "I thank you, my lady."

"Lady Margaret," she said, then turned to introduce her brothers. "My brothers, Lord Hinton and Herbert. I insist you dine with us this forenoon."

Reverend Denning noted the surprise in the eyes of Lord Hinton, who nevertheless hastily added his insistence. The other brother parroted Hinton's welcome. "Yes, please come."

Edward mulled the name. He seldom forgot a name and he tried to pinpoint where he'd heard the name of this woman, whom he was convinced he'd never before seen.

The lady dismissed his sad rig with a hand to her servant. "Bring it around to the hall, Manny.

"Reverend," she said, smiling in a way that made Edward distinctly uncomfortable, "you will ride with us." Taking his arm, she led him to her smart turnout, a white barouche with gold trim. The paneled doors held a freshly painted crest.

Knowing of no way to withdraw without offending the woman, Edward found himself sitting beside her on the long seat with Lord Hinton and Herbert facing them, backs to the horses. The lady kept up a cheerful banter on the way to the family hall designed to relax the visiting clergyman. Edward, however, unaccountably found himself tensing as he frantically searched his mind for the connection to her name. He knew, somehow, it was vital he make the connection.

After a sumptuous luncheon, he followed Lady Margaret and her brothers into a large parlor done ostentatiously in heavy golds, browns and, oddly enough, pink. Like the lady's effusive attitude toward him, it did not fit.

It did not take him long to realize the lady was acting a part for his benefit, a part that amused Lord Hinton and bewildered the younger baby-faced brother. She wanted something from him, but what?

As they sat down on the heavy mahogany furniture, Lady Margaret sighed heavily. Edward sensed it was for his benefit alone. "Is there something wrong, milady?"

She touched his folded hands. "My dear Reverend Denning, I must ask you a question."

"Yes." He tensed.

"Have you a sister named Angella?"

He made the connection. This, then, was the woman Reverend Carter told him the earl bought off in order to pursue his sister. "I do. You know of her?"

A bitter smile twisted the woman's face and for just a moment, the rage that shone from her eyes made Edward start. "*La,* I know of your sister. I am surprised you have not made contact with her since, I understand, you've now been back in England for at least a week or more."

Edward shifted uncomfortably. "I returned to Little Cambrage, but Angella was not there. I understand she was received at Lucashire Hall." He decided not to let on that he knew more. "Might you be able to give me her direction? Afraid Lucashire's man was less than forthcoming with information."

"I am not surprised Lucashire would not wish you to know. I can indeed give you assistance." She clenched her teeth, and seemed to calm herself with some difficulty.

"'Tis not her fault, I suppose, that my erstwhile fiancé is as he is. Never could keep him from dallying with the innocents." She looked up at his face, which he knew had gone decidedly pale, through modestly lowered lashes.

"He picked her up on the outskirts of the village. She came willingly enough." The lady sighed deeply before continuing. "I fear she was quite taken in by my smooth-talking fiancé. Fact is, she was quite besotted with him, and he with her—though these *tendres* of his never last."

"I was told he called off your engagement. Mayhap he had honorable intentions."

Margaret quickly, though unsuccessfully, sought to hide her fury behind the same pitying smile he'd seen on the vicar's full lips. "There was no marriage while we stayed at Lucashire, Reverend Denning." She hesitated. "At no time was there a chaperone present while we resided there. Fact is, Spensor made it clear he would not have one for your sister."

She sighed. "I suppose I must tell you. At times, Herbert is inclined to wander at night."

Herbert looked surprised at this, but Harry kept him from speaking as Margaret continued.

"In looking for him, I happened to look in on the earl's rooms. 'Twas in the middle of the night. I found… well, I hate to shock you, Reverend, but I found your sister with the earl. I might add, she appeared to be right at home there."

Edward frowned. He did not trust the woman overmuch. Like the vicar, she had her own reasons for trying to disgrace Angella. "I understand the earl has presented her to London society. I can't credit a man presenting his mistress as his ward. The scandal alone, should the truth be revealed, would be disastrous."

"You don't know London or the earl. He's a dashing rake. More than likely, he'll pass the whole off as an enormous jest, and get away with it. Men can do things that ruin women for life."

"Yet you do not denounce him."

"No, 'tis more of our secrets, Reverend, though I am sure I may trust your discretion."

He sensed her pause was more for effect than from genuine embarrassment.

"Harry got himself a bit under the hatches so to speak. The earl paid for our silence by buying up Harry's vouchers. For the sake of my family, I can say nothing amiss or the earl will call in Harry's markers. You do understand?"

"I do indeed." Edward's lips tightened. Though he tried to hide it, the anger that flashed in his eyes brought forth a smug smile of satisfaction from Margaret. That gave Edward pause. Something was definitely havey-cavey about the whole. Still and all, what else could he think but that there resided at least some nugget of truth to what the vicar and the lady had told him?

Cutting short his schedule of visits, Edward Denning turned his cattle in the direction of London. Patting his pocket, he made certain he had his mentor's address. As he moved out, he realized with a wry smile, that for all her promises, Lady Ainsworth hadn't given him so much as a farthing for the work, nor had she given Angella's direction.

He well knew her concern for the work had been but a ruse to get him where she might tell him the state of affairs with his sister. For all his rage, he was not such a slow top as not to know she greatly savored her role.

For the next two days he traveled as swiftly as the less-than-prime animals could manage. The fury that tore through him on first hearing the news about his sister was nothing to the rage that consumed him as he entered the bustling city of London.

All around him hawkers cried their wares, the din reminded him sharply of India, where people thronged everywhere. In the cities, the bright-colored saris of the women were a sharp contrast to the somber robes of the pagan monks. He felt more capable of handling his affairs there, far from home, than in dealing with a young woman who had been forced—leastwise he told himself she had been forced—to wantonness for a man who should have protected her.

He considered a thousand plans and discarded each. How was he to approach his sister? If only he knew the whole truth of his sister's circumstances without the vested interests of either of his informants.

And yet, for all his concern for his sister's plight, his thoughts kept turning to a young woman with intense brown eyes.

Chapter 4

"Calm down, Betsy," Angella told her, not for the first time since they had arrived at Lady Obermisst's party.

Betsy grimaced as she tugged on the sleeve of her white silk gown with sprigs of blue and yellow flowers embroidered on the background. "Do you think he'll be here tonight?"

Betsy took note of her friend's momentarily confusion. "Who? Oh, Baron Fritton or the Marquis of Beddinlong."

"Either one, really," Betsy whispered as she plastered on a smile when they entered the room with her mother on one side and her cousin and Angella on the other. "You know I only present well on horseback."

"Nonsense," her mother told her so quietly only their small group heard.

Angella echoed, "Nonsense. Betsy, make this your

night. Make the most of it." Leaning in, she whispered for her ears alone, "Enjoy yourself. Make a conquest or two. If Edward does show up, he'll be jealous."

Betsy exchanged a glance with her friend. "You think mayhap…?"

Angella squeezed her hand. "No, I do not think it likely, though there is no way of knowing. For tonight, at least, do me a favor, all right?"

Betsy glanced over at her friend, almost afraid to agree. What did she have to lose? It wasn't as though Angella would ask of her something outrageous. Hesitantly, Betsy nodded.

"Good," Angella told her. "Now, just for tonight, forget about my brother. Don't let your feelings for him hamper the opportunity of getting better acquainted with other eligible bachelors."

"Like the Marquis of Beddinlong and Baron Fritton?" Betsy surveyed the room, checking to see if either had arrived. She did not see either, but that meant little.

Angella drew her attention back into focus. "Just like the baron and the marquis. Stop worrying so much that you'll trip or appear graceless and concentrate on having a good time. This is a party. Simply enjoy."

Angella asked a hard thing, but why not? She could not do much worse than she had been doing, and besides, Edward wasn't here and could hardly be expected to remember her if he did show up. After all, he was returning to England for his sister, not for a wet-goose young miss who still held a torch for him after formally meeting him but one time—when she was still in the schoolroom. With that, Betsy sighed, put away her dreams, at least temporarily, smiled and nodded firmly.

Angella grinned back as they stepped forward.

Betsy had little more time to consider the matter as they were presented and soon found themselves in a sad crush. She could scarcely hear herself think, much less hope that Baron Fritton might find her, or even wish to do so. Mayhap his request was little more than polite flummery, though she hoped he had more substance than that. Tonight would tell the tale.

Her mother spoke directly into her ear, and still, Betsy scarcely made out the words.

"Lady Obermisst will brag about attendance at this party. Why, she has any number of rooms set aside for dancing, games and food."

Betsy stared around at the opulence of the flecked walls and the magnificent paintings she recognized as the work of great masters. The well-maintained furniture in the different rooms echoed different styles of elegance from Queen Anne and Tudor to Georgian and the romance of Regency.

Betsy stood beside her cousin and Angella as they received congratulations until she wished she were elsewhere. As delighted as she was things turned out for Angella and Spensor, her frustration grew with her own situation. For tonight she moved on, but was it time to let go, permanently, of her dreams of one day meeting Edward again and having him recognize her as a soul mate? By the time Baron Fritton, correct to the shade in tan pantaloons, embroidered waistcoat and a bishop's blue jacket, bowed before her, Betsy was more than ready to take his arm and be led out onto the dance floor.

She found him as nervous as herself about making mistakes and doing something stupid. When he said as much, she spent so much time trying to reassure him, she forgot to be nervous herself. By the time he returned her to her mother's side, she felt quite in charity with him. A new confidence lit her face with a smile.

She found the baron a gentle, kind man who actually listened when she spoke. Something perverse inside pushed her to test him. "While this is all lovely—" she indicated the opulent ballroom, as she continued "—I can't help thinking about all those who scarce provide enough food and clothing for their families."

Betsy knew most of society tried to pretend "those" people did not exist. She tensed, waiting for the baron to brush off the comment with something like "You should not concern your pretty head with such things."

Instead, to her amazement, he shifted from one foot to the other, before answering, "I am comfortable, you understand, not like some…" He hesitated, glanced at Betsy and away as though fearing her response. "To own the truth, I contribute regularly to some of the missions to the poor and needy." He paused, cleared his throat and surveyed Betsy as though gauging her response. "On my estate, I have an orphanage and make sure all employees' children have access to schooling."

Betsy's eyes widened. "I truly am suitably impressed."

"And you think no less of me for my concerns?"

"More actually." Betsy's smile widened as the unpretentious peer soared in her estimation. "Mother, Lady Winter, and I also assist with the needy. In fact, Mother and I often help out at a small London mission." When she mentioned the location, Baron Fritton straightened and paled.

Taking her hand, he spoke with such earnestness Betsy blinked with surprise. "Please tell me you ladies are not so rackety as to go off on your own without escort. It isn't done."

Betsy shook her head, rather enjoying the baron's attentions. "No indeed. Lord Alistair or my cousin Lord Lucashire always accompanies us."

"That is all right, then."

Betsy glowed in the admiration in his gaze as he nodded.

"I would be most happy to offer my services should they be needed."

The two spoke until a broad-shouldered peer cut through the crowd to her side. He bowed. "Miss Carrington."

"Lord Beddinlong."

He held out a hand and drew her to her feet even as he spoke. "You will join me for this country dance, will you not?"

Before she could object or even get nervous, Betsy found herself in the confident arms of the peer. His steps were so sure and his hold so secure, she found herself not worrying about falling at all. All she need do was follow his lead, and he made it easy. By the time the fast country dance was over, Betsy giggled with exhaustion and pleasure. She'd actually had fun. Heady with her success, she allowed the marquis to walk her outside where lanterns lit a beautifully sculpted garden.

The opulence of the house echoed in the carefully trimmed trees and bushes, the Chinese lanterns to light the walkways, the multicolored fountains and the sculpted benches. "This is beautiful!"

She started at the marquis's serious, deep tones. "Not as beautiful as the woman on my arm."

Betsy halted on the pathway. "What!" Was the man

foxed? "What flummery is this? Why, you scarcely know me."

"Ah, but I am getting to know you. Besides, anyone who can handle a horse with the firmness, control and gentleness as you did yesterday is a person I admire, respect…and more."

Betsy blushed as he lowered his voice.

Not used to such flattery, Betsy was at a loss as to how she should go on. Her cousin and Angella saved her from replying as they found her. Stepping forward, Angella took her arm. "Time to come back inside. If you stay much longer, people will talk." Angella winked at Betsy, drawing a blush. "Cannot start gossip, now.…"

Betsy watched the silent interplay between her cousin and the marquis, who backed down quickly. "My apologies, Miss Carrrington. I fear your presence quite set me in such a spin I forgot propriety." He bowed his head toward her. "I trust you will forgive my lapse. Unintended, I assure you."

"*La,* yes, you are forgiven, my lord." Betsy noted her cousin's glare almost with glee. She shot him a grin that brought a look of confusion to his face. Protecting her was on his mind. What tickled Betsy was that this time he tried to protect her because a peer showed marked attention, not because someone was trying to tease her.

Leaning toward Spensor, she murmured, "Thanks, but he meant no harm."

She smiled and agreed when the marquis asked, "I trust you will grace me with another turn on the floor."

Betsy floated through the rest of the evening. With the marked attentions of two eligible bachelors, other eligible bachelors, too, seemed to view her in a more positive light. *Mayhap,* she thought, *it was because, for once, I didn't trip over my own feet.*

With a grimace, Betsy recalled the time her mother decided to hire a tutor to teach her to dance. The tall, gaunt man begged off after two weeks. Betsy overheard the exchange. "I am sorry, Lady Carrington, but your daughter does not have your grace and dignity."

Betsy rolled her eyes and murmured, "Such a toad-eater." She had not cared for him above half, prancing around the room like some fool dandy. He acted as though her inability to keep time to the music were somehow a Cheltenham tragedy. At the time, English lads were dying on foreign land and the instructor acted as though nothing were more important than where she placed her less-than-dainty feet. "Fustian!"

The instructor continued, "I fear your daughter is not ready to apply herself to the niceties of her station. Mayhap when she is ready…" Lady Carrington sent him off with enough to put a smile on his face and the assurance that he would make no mention of her daughter's deficiencies. Betsy bit her lip in frustration. Anger then warred with the feeling inside that she had once more been found wanting.

Her mother, though correct about many things, was not correct about time and maturity changing things for Betsy. Though she was doing better than hoped, she still had a tendency to trip over her own feet at the most awkward of times.

Betsy thought, *Not exactly top of the trees, but not beyond the pale, either. Now, if I just manage not to fall over my feet for the rest of the evening…* Mayhap that instructor would be shocked at her almost grace on the ballroom floor for the entire night.

* * *

Betsy had every intention of holding on to the memory of that perfect night. She figured it would not happen again. Yet the next morning she came down to find cards at the door and visitors, including Fritton and Beddinlong, staying the required half hour. Their conversation was light and fun and, for the first time, Betsy really began to think coming to London hadn't turned out so badly after all.

But late at night her thoughts turned to Edward. Would he think she'd grown too frivolous? Both the baron and the marquis were good men who sought more in a wife than a pretty face. They knew her portion was only passable and did not seem to care. She sensed it would take little for either to declare himself. If she must choose, which spoke more to her heart? Her thoughts returned to Edward. How could she make such a life-changing decision without seeing him first? "Jesus, please help me know what to do."

The next afternoon, her mother asked her to join her and several ladies of her acquaintance.

Betsy headed down the stairs and down the long hall to the south parlor. A manservant opened the door for her. She nodded her thanks. Sucking in a deep breath and praying she would not trip, Betsy entered the room.

To her dismay, all conversation ceased at her entrance. Her foot caught momentarily on the carpet, and for a moment, she panicked, thinking she was going to fall. However, her mother suddenly stood beside her, taking her hands and leading her into the room. She wished her heart would stop beating so loudly. Had she really thought she might be over her awkward stage? Inwardly, she groaned.

"Breathe, Betsy. You are fine. Calm down. Breathe."

She followed the soothing tones of her mother, who spoke too softly for anyone else to hear. More loudly she said, "I would like you ladies to meet my daughter." Lady Carrington turned to Betsy. "Come sit down, dear."

Lady Carrington thrust a plate of sweetmeats into Betsy's hand and poured out tea. Betsy felt the distant rumble in her stomach and hurriedly took a bite of a particular confectionery that happened to be one of her favorites. Her mother wisely let her eat after she nodded and greeted the other women in the room.

Betsy smiled and let the conversation flow around her. The parlor held a warmth that made it one of Betsy's more favored rooms in the Alistair house, outside of the library. The room combined forest-greens and subtle reds on the walls and furnishings, along with delicately carved pediments, that created a warm yet airy feeling about the room. No wonder her mother seemed to prefer it when entertaining guests—some of whom she had not visited with in years.

Betsy soon realized these women had known each other since their own London season many years earlier, if not before. Unexpectedly, the conversation caught her attention.

"Miss Denning's mother's season was a success, yet she chose to marry a man of the cloth," said one lady, shaking her head. Her neck, even during the day, dripped with jewels.

Another in a shockingly yellow gown replied, "But he was a gentleman and quite handsome at that."

"But no prospects." The woman touched the jewels at her throat.

Lady Carrington sipped her tea before replying, "He became the vicar of a living near Lucashire. He was a good man. Too bad about his passing."

Betsy flinched at one lady's less than kindly tone. "Their daughter landed on her feet. Rather a blessing in disguise."

What a way to speak about Angella? How callous of them. The women behaved more like Billingsgate fishwives than gently bred ladies. But for her mother's glance and slight shake of the head, Betsy would have defended her friend. Instead, she bit her lip and listened, curious about Edward and Angella's parents.

"Miss Denning's grandfather disowned her mother for her choice to marry a lowly vicar with no prospects." The woman added, "Though he was from a good family."

Lady Carrington entered the conversation. "Do not seek to fault Miss Denning. Her parentage is better than many who claim society roles."

"True, but then you would defend Lucashire's choice since he is a close connection."

Betsy watched her mother's eyes narrow. The afternoon was not going as her mother had hoped, having tea and conversation with old friends. The women would not be silenced.

"Miss Denning's grandfather is of note," a tall, elegant woman agreed. "He was furious when her mother turned down a marquess for the vicar."

Betsy silently cheered.

The lady in the yellow gown leaned forward. "Did you hear about their son? He was all set to enter the church like his father. Heard tell, his prospects were very good."

The lady with the jewels smiled a sly smile that made Betsy's insides clench. The woman enjoyed her tales much too much. "Instead of cutting a dash in London, the young man, Edward, I think his name is, threw in with the dissenters."

The other ladies sighed almost as one. "No!"

As though, Betsy thought, *choosing other than the state church is tantamount to treason.* She guessed it seemed so for these ladies.

"Baptists," whispered one. "Some missionary called William Carey. Hear tell he went to India." She paused dramatically before continuing with a certain horror in her tone. "To be a missionary to those heathen. I mean…"

Lady Carrington pursed her lips. Betsy knew how much her mother disliked conflict. Yet she sensed her mother did not approve of the direction of the conversation. "Baptist or not, we need good men willing to share God's message with those who've never heard."

The women stopped and stared at her mother as if Lady Carrington had sprouted two heads. Betsy tugged on her sleeve, wishing she could get up and leave. She sensed her mother wished the same. Still, Betsy softened a bit when the women continued gossiping with less venom. Few wished to say ought against her kindly mother.

Betsy knew of William Carey, of course. She'd even read some of his writings. She did not dare explain that Carey's works not only helped draw her closer to Christ, but also turned her purpose from dwelling on her social situation to reaching out to other hurting people.

The woman in yellow asked, "What of Edward Denning? Does he know about his parents…his sister?"

"Indeed." Betsy's mother poured tea into now-empty cups. "The Reverend Edward Denning is even now on his way back to England, mayhap even London."

Edward. The name sounded in her mind and caused her heart to beat a bit more quickly. Now Betsy silently willed the gentlewomen to continue on with this particular topic, but with the gossip aspect spent, they moved on to other revelations.

So much for moving on. Betsy silently vowed to continue to make "Edward" a matter of prayer. If her mother noted her blush, she gave no sign.

"Lord," she prayed later that night after getting ready for bed, "take care of Edward. Bring him home quickly and safely." Once again she thought back to that night where she met him for the first time and he was everything she'd dreamed he would be when she'd first seen his portrait in the family home.

But that was then and now she was in London enjoying a season with Edward's sister. She smiled as she tugged the sleeve of her nightgown in place.

Chapter 5

Angella sank down into a flower-embroidered sofa. "That was quite the walk, Betsy. I fear Baron Fritton would never turn and bring us back. I say, I think he is quite smitten. Yes indeed, quite smitten. Why, he has shown up almost every day to visit or take you for a walk or some such thing."

Betsy wiped sweat from her face. "I can't believe how much I dreaded coming to London, at least until I knew we were going to be brought out together."

She smiled her appreciation as a maid in black gown, white apron and mob cap poured out lemonade for her and Angella. After taking a long sip, she leaned back with a contented sigh. "That is delicious. I'll have to send my compliments to the kitchen."

For a few moments the girls rested. Betsy turned to her friend. "I was so excited when Spensor asked us to come to Lucashire Hall to get reacquainted with you before the season began. *La,* when meeting you again here in London, it was like no time at all had passed since 1805 and your brother's reception when we last spoke with each other.

"I was excited about coming to London, but not so much the reason. We both know where my heart lies, but I also felt—and still feel to some extent—I need to find an eligible *parti* to assure Mother she need not worry about my future."

"Now, with at least two gentlemen at your feet, what do you think of the season?"

Betsy sucked in a deep breath and opted for honesty. "Excitement, confusion…hope."

Tugging down her sleeve, Betsy stared into her glass. "The season is not turning out so bad after all. I mean, I had visions of stumbling, tripping, falling…so far… not too bad."

Angella took off her shoes and rubbed her feet. "I know. Not the thing to do, but those shoes hurt. Next time, I'll let you walk alone with one of the maids as chaperone."

"No. Wear different shoes." Betsy raised her hand. "I don't want to be out walking alone. Not even with the baron, sweet man that he is."

Angella's expression showed confusion. "Certainly you do not fear Fritton. Never saw a gentleman so eager to please."

Betsy rolled her eyes. "A bit too much, if you ask me."

"You don't care for him, then?"

"Yes. No. I don't know." Betsy tugged at the sleeve of her rose muslin gown in her agitation. With a start,

Betsy realized that, since coming to London, she had started doing so whenever she was upset or agitated. Instead, she smoothed down the wrinkle she'd created.

Though Betsy averted her face, she felt Angella's gaze. "Um. Mayhap you have more of a partiality for the marquis. He thinks you are top drawer, especially on the back of a horse."

"I do like him well enough, I suppose, though I scarcely can say I know him. I do like that he doesn't care a fig whether I have a goodly portion or not. Said he is well enough placed, and for him, such things don't matter."

"I see."

Betsy heard a world of unspoken thoughts in Angella's words.

"So, has he spoken for your hand, mayhap?"

Betsy flushed and glanced at her friend. There was no gainsaying Angella. "All right. He has hinted around the subject."

Angella pursed her lips. "But you haven't given him sufficient reason to pursue the subject?"

Betsy shrugged. "I don't know. I just don't know, Angella."

She knew her friend read her distress, for Angella took her hand and squeezed it. "I do so want you to find someone. I know you have a partiality for my brother, but I do not want you to set your heart on him. He's been gone for so long…"

Betsy pulled away. "Don't you think I know that? But…"

Angella nodded. "I know. You need to be sure." Angella sighed. "Then we'd best pray my brother shows up before that decision needs to be made."

At that moment, Betsy's mother entered the room. She tucked a stray strand of hair under her broad hat as she surveyed the girls. "Alistair says he has time to take us down to the mission after lunch. What about it, girls? We'll all be far too busy tomorrow with your coming-out ball, Betsy." Her expression held a certain smugness that made Betsy cringe. "I think at least two bachelors... and more will be at the ready for the evening."

Betsy clapped her hands over her burning cheeks. "Really, Mother."

Angella got to her feet. "Come on, Betsy, let's change for our afternoon at the mission." They had started wearing their older fashions to that part of town for their own safety.

Betsy did not need be told twice. She was eager to escape her mother's speculation.

While the time at the mission was rewarding, Betsy could not help being excited about her ball. A party put on for her and her alone. The thought was heady indeed.

Her gown was everything she could have imagined as it sparkled in the light of the crystal chandeliers, candelabrum and the myriad lit candles situated around the room decorated with fresh flowers in silver bowls. The dressmaker had done wonders with the gown and lace overlay that fit her thin figure to perfection. Betsy actually felt graceful in the gown, at least more graceful than usual. Her mother surprised her with a delicate emerald and diamond necklace.

Her cousin, very much the aristocratic gentleman in a black superfine coat, gray waistcoat and black breeches, led her out in the first dance. His smile was gentle and proud as he held her. "You look beautiful, Betsy. You will certainly turn heads tonight." He grinned. "Here tell you've already turned some heads." He winked. "Good for you. You've come a long way from the insecure child who tried to hide away on my grand birthday celebration."

Betsy's expression tightened with the memory. "Yes, but as always, you left your guests to hide away with me for a time in the barn." She patted the shoulder of his jacket. "You did not care a fig whether or not you got your clothing, even then the first stare of fashion, dirty." A smile touched her lips and faded. "I do not know what I would have done without you in my life, Spensor, especially after Father….after Father…passed on."

Lucashire's hold tightened. "Losing him so unexpectedly in that accident was dreadful for you, for all of us who cared for and admired him." He leaned closer to whisper in her ear, "He would be proud of you tonight, Betsy. You are all that is kind, gentle, good…and you are managing to stay on your feet." His quick change startled Betsy into giving him a slight shove.

"Hey. It is true. You should be proud of yourself." She followed his gaze to where Baron Fritton slapped his gloves against his palm nervously and where the marquis danced with an older woman with a gown of shocking red that did not set off her rather rotund figure well. The sight made Betsy cringe until she caught the gaze of the marquis, who nodded.

With the dance completed, Lucashire held out his arm to escort her back to her mother. Spensor pulled her attention back to him. "You may not have taken all of London by storm, but it appears you do have a couple of serious suitors."

Betsy blushed. "Oh, Spensor, such stuff and non-sense."

As they moved slowly through the packed crowd, his eyebrow lifted. "Really, now. Doing it up a bit much, are we not? Do not forget, I've seen the young Fritton groveling and have spoken with the marquis." His expression grew serious. "I think both are serious contenders for your hand, and there are others waiting should you offer encouragement."

"Spensor, it is almost too much. This is a dream, so different from your birthday party. I was an antidote."

"No," Lucashire said, his lips firm, "they were unnecessarily cruel. But now, this spring in London, you're coming into your own." With a flourish and a bow, he landed her back beside her mother before commenting, "There is a new confidence about you. I like seeing your smile."

His words lifted Betsy as nothing else could have and she floated through the evening. She relished her role as belle of the ball and danced and laughed and never stumbled once. The attention of two contenders and many other would-be contenders was heady indeed. She was not such a green head not to realize some of those showing attention were desperate for a bride with even a respectable, if not overly abundant, portion.

She grinned as Angella danced by in the arms of Spensor, both so caught up in each other, they scarce noticed her. The expression on her mother's face was one of triumph. Betsy could almost read her thoughts. "My daughter has done well."

The marquis bowed before her, asking to escort her to supper. As she accepted, she noticed the baron close behind him, his expression stricken. Her heart went out to him. With a smile she stepped forward and tucked her hand through the arms of both. "Why don't both you fine gentlemen escort me to supper?"

Fritton gasped and grinned, pleasure written all over his face. The marquis glowered, but dipped his head in acknowledgment. With two such different companions, supper proved interesting and fun as they touched on all manner of subjects, from the marquis's favorite subject of horses, racing and breeding to Fritton's concern for the needy and farm management. The two men managed to stay civil.

Betsy sent up thanks the other women at their table refrained from posing on the latest gossip. She sent the marquis a glance of approval when he diverted the men whenever they drifted into discussing the recent war with either Napoleon or the colonies. She always cringed at the tendency to spread the on dits, knowing how quickly one could become the subject of nasty gossip and rumour.

As conversation eddied around her, Betsy surveyed the two men at her side. With a suddenness that took her by surprise, she realized their attentions, while exciting, were not part of a game. These men came to London to court and marry. They wanted companions, children and heirs. From her admittedly short acquaintance, she knew the men spent most of the year on their estates and took their responsibilities seriously—and that included finding a mate.

Would either or both offer for her? Betsy studied Fritton as she smiled and spoke to him. Tall and thin like herself, he had once been as picked on as she had been herself, she sensed. Yet he'd grown into a sweet, gentle man who would make a woman proud. Betsy searched her heart. What did she feel for the caring young man? Friendship. Yes, she cared about him true enough, but more.... With insight, she admitted to herself he reminded her more of the younger brother she always wished she had than the suitor he wished to become. With a sigh, Betsy turned to the marquis.

About that time others stood and headed back to the dance floor. She had little time to assess the situation before finding herself on the arm of the marquis, who escorted her out into the garden. While this garden was not the first style of elegance of the sculpted garden where she first walked with the marquis, the Alistair garden allowed for a wide variety of wildflowers in the more restrained space.

He placed a hand over hers tucked in his elbow. "Time we leave the cub behind, my dear. You are kindness itself, but he is not for you."

Betsy sighed, not sure whether to be relieved he understood or irritated the man took so much for granted. For a time they strolled along in silence. Betsy breathed in the fragrance of the flowers and listened to the gentle rustling of the trees around them. Her special night had turned into more of a success than she had anticipated.

At least two of the gentlemen who approached her tonight belonged to the young peers who had teased her younger self for her awkwardness. There was no time for recriminations tonight, especially not since one actually stuttered an apology. The other acted as though he never met her before. Mayhap he really did not recall his cruel childhood antics. Betsy glanced upward. Peace pervaded her heart and she smiled. It was time to release the hurt of the past. *Thank You, Lord.*

"Betsy. Betsy." The marquis's tone drew her back. "Where have you gone?"

She blushed, scrambling for something to explain. "This is a perfect night. So peaceful, quiet."

"Glad I can make you feel that way."

Betsy bit her lip, not wishing to explain he was not the reason. Her silence seemed to encourage him. In the shadow of a large tree, the marquis turned her to face him. Taking her hands, he stared down into her face with such intensity Betsy glanced away. It surprised her how much light the lanterns hung around the garden offered. Even in the yellowish shadows, she made out his features.

His voice held a hint of hesitation that surprised her and brought her gaze back to the marquis's face. "Please tell me you are not seriously considering the young baron as a suitor."

"I was." Betsy bit her lip. "Mayhap… It is not as though I need decide now. Yet…"

"So what changed your mind?"

Betsy felt the grip of his hands and the sweat even through his gloves. So the man wasn't as sure as he let on. Her response mattered to him. The thought that any man considered her response so seriously quite set her head in a spin. The marquis, who knew what he was about and who knew what he sought in a wife, thought her smack up to the mark.

Somehow the cant phrasing of her thoughts brought a slight smile to her lips. Then a frown as she forced her mind back to the matter at hand. Fritton. She liked him well enough, even considered him a friend. But more… Betsy did not even want to imagine him kissing her.

"Do not tell him so. He is a dear man, but…but,"

Betsy finally confessed, "he's more like a friend or brother to me. I fear that is all he shall ever be—a friend." Betsy gazed up at the marquis. "Please do not tease him about this." She sighed. Matters of the heart were difficult to negotiate without hurting feelings. "I wish to speak to him myself about the matter should he choose to approach me."

"I understand, Miss Carrington. I am not so rag-mannered as to crush his expectations."

Betsy colored. "I did not mean to imply…"

The marquis touched her face, lightly, gently, causing Betsy's heart to flutter. She wished it was Edward's hand touching her face instead, Edward's face gazing down at her with intense gentleness and more. But the marquis stood beside her, not Edward.

A wry smile crossed the marquis's face. "I know."

Betsy leaned forward. "I appreciate your sensitivity on this manner."

For a moment the nobleman regarded her. "No, I would not wish to distress him or you in such a fashion."

Betsy refrained from hugging the man. He would not only think her manners to let, but also would probably consider her behavior forward. He might well read more into her response than intended. Betsy tugged at her sleeve, silently decrying the restrictions of polite society. "Thank you, my lord."

The marquis frowned. "However, Miss Carrington, I did not bring you out here to speak of Fritton or any other man for that matter. I have come to care for you, Miss Carrington." He paused as though judging her response, before continuing. "I came to ask if there is any hope for my suit."

Betsy gulped. Her stomach churned. What could

she say, should she say? What was the truth? She enjoyed spending time in his company. While he was a supreme horseman and followed the races, he had more depth than the recitation of the bloodlines of racing horse favorites.

They shared a love of good books, though she'd not confessed her love of those scandalous novels by Mrs. Radcliff. Though many women of society read them, most who did pretended no knowledge of such works. Why they focused on romance and love and dangerous situations rather than dry literary topics. Betsy bit her lip to keep a smile from her lips.

It would not do to make the marquis feel she mocked his suit or took his manner less than seriously. She shifted from one foot, now going to sleep, to the other. She'd rather walk, but the marquis held her attention as he pressed his suit.

The marquis had been all that was kind and gentlemanly. He was a fine figure of a man—on and off a horse. Betsy sighed. Here was a good man, a man she could trust. Furthermore, Spensor had all but given his approval to such a match if the marquis came up to scratch. He said the marquis conducted himself with integrity without the vices of many peers. From her cousin's expression, she knew this included his own antics not so long past.

Still and all, instead of being excited and breathless at the implications, Betsy felt trapped.

For a moment she scolded herself. Marriage would please her mother and ensure that both of them would not need worry about finances in the foreseeable future. And yet…how could she sell herself for simply a comfortable position in society? No!

Betsy's heart cried out to the one man who held her heart. *Oh, Edward!* It was not as though he pursued her or wrote to her or in any way indicated he wished for a wife. But he was coming to London. She would see him again. Then she would know, wouldn't she?

Still and all, she was not ready to entrust another man with her heart. *Lord,* she cried out silently, *where are You in this?*

Her silence prompted the marquis to repeat his question with less confidence. Betsy took his arm. "My dear marquis. You are a kind and good man. Any woman would be honored..."

"But not you, Betsy?"

She sensed his masked hurt.

She glanced up at him and away. "I wish...I wish I could feel for you the way the woman you choose should feel. I do care for you." She hesitated. "Truth be told, we scarcely know each other."

Yet had she not fallen for Edward not when they met, but when she first viewed his portrait? She'd spent far more time with the marquis than she'd ever been able to spend with Edward, and still something bound her to him. With the marquis all but declaring himself, why couldn't she forget Edward and love a man like the marquis?

He had the qualities she looked for—a man who cared about his people and estates, a horseman who wasn't afraid to compliment a woman with similar skills, a man of faith and integrity and a man other men respected. In their talks even on such short acquaintance, Betsy realized she'd learned quite a lot about the man. Anger simmered. If she had not gone with Angella to the vicarage that night, she would never have seen that family picture.

Betsy was honest enough to admit that would have made little difference when she met Edward at his reception on completion of his studies. She sighed. Such a tangle and her stomach knotted.

"You might grow to care, Miss Carrington." Hope flashed in his eyes.

Biting her lip, Betsy swallowed. "I would like to think so, but to own the truth, I cannot say time would make a difference."

His eyes narrowed in thought. "There is someone else. But if not Fritton, who?"

Betsy smiled then, a small sad smile that ended in a long sigh. "Sometimes we cannot dictate where our hearts take us—even when we might wish elsewise."

"Then you are not yet spoken for?"

Betsy shook her head. "No, nor am I sure of anything."

When she witnessed growing confidence in his eyes, Betsy wished she had been less forthright when he told her, "Sometimes the heart can be persuaded, my dear."

"I cannot give you encouragement, my lord."

At that moment, they were interrupted, leaving Betsy in a world of confusion.

Chapter 6

The Reverend Avery Jeremiah welcomed Edward profusely. "Come in. Come in, lad. Did not think you were due in London for some time yet."

Edward felt a twitch start in his cheek. "Yes, well, there were circumstances that necessitated moving up my schedule."

"I see."

Edward felt the man's gaze and shifted uncomfortably. His mentor always did have the ability to see beneath the surface. Reverend Jeremiah reminded him sharply of his father, and he felt a pain deep inside that he'd never again see his father this side of Heaven. The minister's response held a world of questions, and Edward knew the man would seek to discover the reason for the truncated schedule.

Edward was more than happy to put his things in his

room and relax a moment or two. It turned into more. In the place where he'd spent so many happy hours as a student, Edward, for the first time since arriving in England, fell into a deep, dreamless slumber.

When he awoke, surprisingly refreshed, he sat up and noticed his clothes had been pressed and laid out by Jeremiah's manservant. In India, Edward had learned to wake at the slightest movement or sound. Away from the compound, he had learned not to let down his guard. Danger lurked from nature—animal and human.

Many did not care for the gospel of love and hope he and his fellow missionaries shared. He shuddered at the thought of what some native religions practiced. Riffling his fingers through his blond hair, Edward sighed and rose to his feet to wash and dress. Here he let down his guard and it felt…good.

He rose more refreshed than, than… He frowned. In truth, he had not felt so rested since long before the letter arrived from Angella. William Carey had been correct, as usual. Edward had needed a break, needed time to reconnect with his past, his family, his home.

Did his stubbornness cause the situation with his sister? The thought was not to be borne. With a deep sigh, he began to dress. He knew when dinner was served. His mentor set a routine that had not been altered in all the years Edward had been in London studying for the ministry.

Edward stopped just inside the double doors to the dining hall. The full table was not a surprise. Reverend Jeremiah enjoyed filling his table with students, pastors, bishops and missionaries from different persuasions. Edward recalled, with a slight smile, the energetic conversions and discussions of faith, politics and more around the table laden with enough food to keep even the ever-hungry students satisfied.

However, it wasn't the memories that kept him rooted to the spot. For a man who gave little consideration to his clothing, that is exactly why he hesitated. Even the students who, from his own experience, he knew scarcely had a pence to fly with wore clothing that made his look shabby by comparison. He noted that the cut of the jackets had changed since he'd left for India, and many even wore long pants instead of breeches. He had all but decided to back out of the room when the minister noticed him and waved him into the room. Getting up, Jeremiah offered him an empty seat to his right— a place of honor.

There was little Edward could do but accept graciously. He nodded as Jeremiah embarrassed him with praise. For that evening Edward was able to force aside his primary reason for returning to England and for his trip to London and speak of his missionary work in India.

For all his eloquence and warmth toward him, Edward sensed his host was astute enough to sense something amiss. After the guests departed and the students were either out with friends or studying in their rooms, Jeremiah sat down with Edward in the parlor.

"What is it, Edward? What's bothering you?" The older man's solicitude broke Edward's reserve.

Haltingly he explained the situation. He finished with a question. "I cared not for either the vicar or Lady Margaret by half, but might they speak the truth of the matter?" Almost of its own volition another followed. "How could Lucashire…or Angella…?"

Though Edward took care not to vent his frustration on the clergyman, he realized the minister heard the undertone of rage. With concern, the man surveyed the younger man. He remained silent for so long, he discomfited Edward.

"Have I greatly misread the situation? What am I to do?"

Getting to his feet, his mentor told him, "Stop. Pray. Meditate. Listen. Wait. Discover the truth of the matter. See if there's any truth in the charges leveled against either the Earl of Lucashire or your sister. What you heard may have all been a hum. You have good reason to doubt those two talebearers. Don't do anything foolish. We'll find the truth. Meanwhile, I can use you here."

Edward glanced down at his worn jacket. "I fear that most of what I have is scarce presentable." His lips twisted ruefully. "Not exactly slap up to the mark."

His host laughed. "Never you mind about that. I'll fix you up right and tight. Styles have changed, lad. Pantaloons are in every man's wardrobe these days."

"I cannot let—"

"Lad, you cannot stop me from doing what I wish to do." He paused. "Consider the starched-up nobs who have the blunt to assist in your work. How you present yourself does matter." The man paused again. "Edward. Think of a new wardrobe as part of my support."

Edward knew from experience there was no gainsaying his mentor. He merely nodded.

With that handled, the minister reverted to the situation with Angella. "Edward, I see you still struggle with anger. It does no good and halts rational thought. Rein in that temper long enough to discover the truth of the matter. Then we can decide how best to proceed. Until you properly deal with this situation, you cannot fully put your mind to your calling."

Edward soon found himself fitted for clothes, which better fit his lean frame and were more in fashion than those he'd brought back with him from India. Edward's mentor and friend allowed him little time to lie around and mope about the situation he might find with his sister. Almost every evening, students, pastors and professors filled the mentor's table. The discussions and debates were lively and challenging, though the mentor never allowed those discussions to get out of hand or to descend into personal attacks.

In the semi-isolation of his work in India, where he often ministered with little support and certainly none of the caliber of interaction he found in London, Edward realized he'd let his critical thinking skills lapse. He now enjoyed the challenge and thrust of the exchanges. He also found himself going back to the Word to dig for truth and to discover if mayhap some of his positions needed some adjustment.

He began to truly understand the need for fellowship and how easy it was to isolate yourself. It was not healthy. He had indeed needed to return to England and was glad for Reverend Jeremiah's quiet teaching.

At times, and though the minister refused to admit to it, Edward sensed he chose the company with him in mind. Other times, he accompanied the minister on a round of meetings, events and ministry opportunities. He found himself sharing about his work in small unpretentious chapels and in opulent drawing rooms with the cream of the ton. He felt comfortable in the first setting and out of place in the second, but he gave thanks his background and training helped him present himself credibly at either venue.

Regardless of the location or the status of the audience, before speaking Edward sent up a prayer for wisdom. When he concentrated on telling stories about his work in India, he found both audiences responded. As he spoke about his work in opulent parlors filled with individuals and couples with an array of titles, he found some interested, some asking to assist financially because they believed in what he was doing and some who agreed to donate because, Edward suspected, they wanted to appear generous and self-sacrificing. Edward did not care what the motivation. He was grateful for whatever help they offered.

"I really need to spend time looking for my sister," he told his mentor as they headed out to another speaking engagement.

For a moment, the minister said nothing. "You've had any number of opportunities, Edward. Have you considered your sister or Lucashire might well attend one of the events at which you speak?"

He paused before urging the horse into a faster gait. "Mayhap they will find you."

Edward kept himself from slapping his forehead. "Of course. I should be on the lookout for them when I'm out with you." So far, nothing had come of it, but from then on Edward kept his eyes open for anyone who resembled an older version of the young girl he once protected from village bullies.

He couldn't help also looking around for the face of the woman whose image refused to leave his thoughts. In fact, since arriving in London, Edward found that Betsy often inhabited his dreams—pleasant dreams.

Not many days hence, the thick London air and city congestion started to bother Edward, so used to wide-open places and clean air. Again he accompanied Reverend Jeremiah to speak about his work. Truth be told, he would rather have stayed home and rested. Edward was weary, deep down, and the schedule he was keeping did not help. He yawned behind his hand, noting the slight smile on Reverend Jeremiah's face.

"Do not say anything, Reverend Jeremiah. Even now you have more stamina than most students."

They chatted then about inconsequential things, marking time as they traveled. The carriage was well sprung and the horse frisky and moving as quickly as the pastor allowed.

The afternoon sun beat down hot and bright, a nice change from the chill and fog that often enveloped London. At times, Edward had the urge to ride out into the countryside just to breathe in fresh, clean air and not the stale congestion of the city. He sighed. That would probably not happen until his mission was complete—to find his sister and get her settled someplace safe. That, too, remained a bit of a puzzle, though the pastor promised to assist him in that regard when the time came to do so. For that he was grateful.

The location to which they drove was not an easy find, and Edward sensed even his mentor was getting a bit restive over the time lost in heading in one wrong direction after another. "It should not be that difficult to find," the pastor said, not for the first time. The horse nodded as though in agreement, blowing and leaning into the harness.

Edward cleared his throat. "Would you wish me to inquire at one of these establishments or houses?"

He waited more than a heartbeat or two for the older man to reply. "Not...yet. We still have time."

Edward swallowed a grin. As much as he admired and respected the older pastor, he also recalled ramming into his stubborn side a time or two. The man prided himself on knowing London. Not finding the address had to dearly vex him.

Two turns later, they came upon a carriage listing seriously to one side. A tall gentleman with windswept hair lifted a petite woman from the vehicle along with two young boys. The pastor drove up beside them. "Might we be of assistance?"

The man's gray eyes assessed them. "Seems our carriage wheel was loose. Needs to be fixed before we can continue."

Edward was used to fending for himself in the countryside of India. "I could help with the repairs."

"That would be most appreciated." The gentleman walked over to them. The pastor nodded first to the gentleman and then the lady. "Lord Alistair. Lady Alistair."

Alistair smiled. "You have me at a disadvantage."

The pastor introduced himself and turned toward Edward. At that moment, one of the horses, uneasy at the restraint on his bridle by the coachman at his head, threw up his head. The coachman, not expecting the move, was flung to one side. That in turn caused both lead horses to start and pull forward, putting them all at risk.

In a thrice, Edward leaped from the vehicle to the horses and grabbed the harness. With soft words, he quickly had them calmed. The coachman, unhurt but rubbing his shoulder, took back control. "Thank you, sir. Caught me wrong, there."

Alistair echoed his thanks. Edward discovered Alistair was no starched-up peer. He put his efforts as much as did Edward in tightening the wheel and making sure the carriage was ready for travel. "We're heading out of town for a few days, so I appreciate the quick assistance." Alistair handed his wife and sons back into the carriage before one last thank-you.

He clasped Edward's hand. "If there is ought you need, we'll be back in town in a week, two at the most. Find us at Alistair House."

Edward thought of Angella. If he had not found her direction by the time Lord Alistair returned, mayhap the man would assist Edward in finding her. Now was not the time to ask. Instead, he motioned toward the pastor. He asked after the address they sought. Lord Alistair provided clear directions.

Edward and his mentor watched the carriage head out of sight. With Alistair's directions, they had little trouble locating the hall.

As they reached their destination, Edward glanced over at the pastor. "I don't think that was happenstance."

The pastor prepared to step down, stopped and surveyed Edward. "No, it wasn't and, I am convinced, for more reasons than we even realize."

Edward tried to figure out what his mentor meant as he followed him into the building.

A couple of days later, Reverend Jeremiah approached him about another matter entirely. "Our congregation helps support a small work in a less-than-prosperous part of town."

Edward's eyebrows rose at the location—one of the least desirable places a person wanted to find himself in. He'd worked at missions in those areas before he left for India while he was still in school. The needs were so great. Young women had little recourse but to sell themselves for a scrap of bread. Children, scarcely more than toddlers really, begged on the street corners. Starvation in the villages of deprived India was one thing, but it was criminal to find such deprivation, even starvation, in the land where more food was wasted at some dinners given by Prinny than several families could eat in a month. It was frustrating, infuriating and horrible. "I take it you can use my involvement. Whatever you ask, I will do my best. As long as I have opportunity to find my sister's direction."

That's how Edward found himself driving a worn, old-fashioned rig with a gray horse that had seen better days toward a part of town that gave him pause. No one with any sense would drive a new vehicle down there or dress in the mode. It was best to blend in as much as possible. Fortunately, his clothes from India were perfect for this assignment.

It wasn't a place anyone went alone, but he had no other choice. Before Edward left, his mentor had handed him a small pistol that now resided in his pocket. He clucked and shook the reins enough to keep the gray going at a pace that kept them ahead of the mongrel dogs eying them from the side of the roadway.

The animal was amiable enough and worked in the harness with a will. He passed by fancy carriages, cabriolets and other smart turnouts. Even the servant drivers of the rigs turned up their noses at his less-than-fashionable getup. Where he was headed, fashionable was not a positive word and would only pose danger.

He left behind the wider streets for narrow, rutted ways that could scarcely be called roads. Large, imposing mansions gave way to modest dwellings. As he turned down another street, odors assailed Edward's nose. The smells of rotted food and unwashed bodies mingled with those of unsanitary conditions. The upper crust, thanks to Brummel, had revolutionized their concept on cleanliness, and the nobility now regularly bathed and wore clean clothes. Those conditions did not apply to this segment of the population.

Water was not readily available and filth piled up in the troughs beneath the shacks whose owners probably called houses. It reminded Edward sharply of India, and strangely enough, he missed his work, missed his people. He did not belong in England. Not anymore. Still and all, he must discover the truth about Angella and make certain to see to her future. That was worry enough.

His thoughts turned to the young woman, Betsy, he'd met so long ago. He hoped to see her, as well, before he returned to India. He had little to offer any woman, especially one as fine as the woman whom he couldn't get out of his mind or, when he was honest, his heart. Nonetheless, he had a compulsion to look her up if she was indeed in London.

"Lord, are You in this?" He shook his head. What a strange prayer. Of course, God was in control of everything. Frowning, Edward pulled the gray to one side and stopped. By now he should have arrived at what his mentor described as a small, unpretentious white clapboard building with a cross on the front.

Pulling out a piece of parchment paper on which the pastor had written the directions, Edward checked it while keeping an eye out for the mangy dogs creeping toward his rig. He turned a street too soon. Tucking the paper back into his pocket, Edward took up the reins. While he didn't usually use the whip, he used it now as a threat to two black-and-white half-starved mutts that managed to get within a couple of feet of the horse.

Recognizing danger, the gray flipped its ears back toward him and shifted nervously. The animal eagerly, seemingly almost relieved, headed out in a trot. Turning his vehicle about, Edward found his way to the right street. Ahead was the mission exactly like what his mentor had described. As he drove up, a young woman was struggling with a man, wearing a fashionable top coat, who had little business being in this part of town.

"Let me go!" The woman pushed against the man, who almost lost his hold. Cursing, he grabbed her arm with so much force, she cried out in pain.

Though Edward had no notion of who the woman was, he could not stand by and allow any woman to be so treated. "I say, sir. Let her go."

Realizing he was being observed, the man grunted. "She's mine. Get your own girl. They're on every street corner."

At this the young woman turned crimson. Her eyes widened. "I am not one of your girls or any girl, for that matter. Now let me go."

Even at that distance, Edward took note of the woman's tense, resisting body.

"No other sort would be in this place," the man reasoned. He began all but dragging her along with him. Edward saw a closed carriage up the street. The fashionable turnout revealed much to Edward. How many peers sought their less-than-genteel pleasures down here far from their families and the wagging tongues of polite society? Most turned a blind eye to such goings-on, claiming, "Men will be men."

The absolute terror on the woman's face forced Edward to action. Without considering further, he slapped the reins and aimed the horse down the street. The man had the woman halfway across, while she dragged her feet, fighting every inch of the way. The woman's attire was not that of a woman of a certain stamp. Did not the man realize she was attired as a gently bred female? Apparently not. He suspected the peer was a bit bosky.

He was not a great whip, so he lifted up a prayer. "Help me do this, Lord, please."

Driving up next to the peer and the young woman, he held out his hand and yanked the young woman practically into his lap. The man stumbled back.

The woman yelped and scrambled out of Edward's lap onto the seat beside him as he drove down the road.

"Who are you?" She looked only slightly less frightened than before as she tried to straighten her jacket and skirt. She glanced at the ground as though contemplating a jump.

Edward reached out to hold her arm. "Miss, please, I'm trying to rescue you from that scoundrel."

She stared at him a moment. "Thank you, sir." As she turned, her eyes widened. "Oh no! He's following us."

Edward's stomach clinched. He glanced back. Sure enough, the man had climbed onto the driver's box and had set the horses into a trot. He was close enough that Edward could see the glower on the man's face. Curses poured from the man's mouth. The nobleman's driver hung on to the seat beside him as the carriage headed directly toward Edward. The man had no intention of letting his comely piece escape.

Edward slapped the reins against the back of the gray. Thankfully, the animal responded. A moment later, the horse's ears flicked back and he jumped into a faster gait. Faster was not good on the rutted road. Yet there was no gainsaying that the peer had every intention of running into them. Edward felt his light rig rise as the gray responded to the thunder of the racing carriage.

Though his gig was more lightweight than the carriage, it had seen much wear, while the carriage was well sprung with fresh, eager horses.

The young woman clung to the seat, her face stunned into silence and fear. "Save us, God. Please save us," he heard her mutter, and he echoed the sentiment.

A moment later, they exploded into the main thoroughfare. Edward was able to maneuver into the traffic and away from the peer, who was cut off by a lumbering wagon. With a quick glance behind him, Edward turned down one street and then another.

Finally he pulled up the gray, who was blowing and wheezing. He found his own breath expelling in gulps and heaves. Catching his breath, he turned to the young woman beside him.

"I think you're safe now, miss."

Suddenly he sucked in a deep breath as he stared into the deep brown eyes he'd dreamed about since his reception at Lucashire Hall. "Betsy?" He felt the nervous tic in his left cheek. "I mean, Carrington, Miss Elizabeth Carrington… Oh dear, you know who you are." If humiliation could open a hole, he'd gladly jump in. Instead, he simply fell embarrassingly silent.

Chapter 7

Betsy stared at the handsome man beside her who had gone out of his way to rescue her from that rake, that, that rakehell, that scapegrace. Oh, she ran out of nasty things to call the peer who thought she was some sort of lightskirt and tried to force her… And in front of the mission at that.

How dare he not listen when she told him she was not what he was looking for—a woman of pleasure? She felt her cheeks heat and covered them with her hands. Her body felt bruised all over. She tugged skirt, top and jacket back into some semblance of respectability.

Anger bubbled inside as well as myriad other emotions she could not properly name at the moment. She blushed just thinking about what might have happened had not the dark, serious man beside her stepped in.

She surveyed the man in a well-cut, if not quite in

the latest fashion jacket. His worn boots were nonetheless polished to a high shine.

Her plans had gone very badly wrong and she knew, unless she could sneak home undetected, everyone from her mother to her cousin would ring a regular peal over her poor head. Betsy sighed.

The man beside her looked vaguely familiar and he certainly seemed to know her. Blast it anyway! Though not tall like her cousin, her rescuer was at least her height, thin, with wavy blond hair and startling blue eyes that stared back at her in stunned surprise. Was he ever going to speak again?

"You know who I am?" It was the best she could manage under the circumstances.

He nodded. "I do. Did. Uh." A slight, crooked smile turned up his lips, taking the frown from his face and making him quite handsome. "I'm not usually so tongue-tied, but you there were a surprise."

Betsy supplied. "Shock, more like."

He swallowed, coughed. "Glad I could be of service." He glanced around. "I think we lost him. When he sobers up, he might have little recall of the events of the last few minutes."

"We can certainly hope so." Betsy's sentiment was more than a little hopeful. Anxiety clutched her insides. "What if he doesn't and meets me elsewhere?"

"I doubt the man would wish to admit his activities in this part of town." His lips turned up slightly. "Miss Carrington—it is Carrington, is it not? Miss Carrington, he is not going to recognize you at any society events, of that you can be certain."

That smile. She'd seen that smile before. She wrinkled her forehead in thought. The shape of the face, the smile, a picture. Her thoughts, prayers…dreams. *Oh my!* Betsy almost fell off the rig as she recognized her rescuer. "Oh no! Edward? Edward Denning?"

He did as courtly a bow as their position allowed. "At your service, miss."

"Betsy," she told him. "Just Betsy."

He gulped. Nodded. "B…Betsy."

She sighed. "At least, I know I am safe enough in your care."

He straightened. "I should hope so, but what were you doing—alone—down by that mission?"

Betsy squirmed in her seat. "Well, I…"

Horror flashed on Edward's face. "Are you saying you deliberately went there alone?"

She could see how the very idea upset her rescuer.

Imagine, being rescued by the man she'd been dreaming about and praying for positively *years*. Maybe God was in this. She sent up a plea. *God?* Oh, but what a dilemma. He'd take her directly back to Alistair House and talk to her mother and cousin. Of course, maybe he did not know where his sister was.

Frowning, Edward repeated, "Tell me you did not go there alone."

"All right, I took a cab to the mission. Yes." She quailed under his glare and gulped. "Please let me explain. I—I had good reason. Oh, botheration! Mother and Winter were out and about and…" She stopped before saying anything about Angella. She shrugged. "No one else was about to escort me, so I took a hackney cab." His silence unnerved her. "I—someone needed to be at the mission. There was no one else, you understand." She grabbed the seat as the gray chose that moment of Edward's inattention on the reins to shake his head and stretch out his nose.

Betsy gulped again, waiting for Edward's response. She felt a frisson of anger building at his icy gaze. Her all-too-recent run-in with the peer, her rescue and her reasons for going to the mission whirled in her mind. She well knew the response she would receive once Angella, Spensor and Lord and Lady Alistair, not to mention her mother, discovered the truth of the matter. Her stomach churned as she waited for Edward to speak.

Edward put a light hand on the reins to halt the gray as the animal shifted and took a few steps forward. He glanced at her and away. He cleared his throat. When he focused his attention on her, she felt her throat close and swallowed. "What a noddycock thing to do. Have you windmills in your head?"

Whatever she expected, it was not that set-down. Betsy tensed and ground her teeth as her temper rose. Whoever did he think he was—her keeper? "I have not." Her eyes flashed. "Mr., I mean, Reverend Edward Denning, you have no call to say such things to me, you… you… Oh, I don't know what you are."

Sarcasm twisted the man lips. "I, Miss Betsy Carrington, am the man, you might recall, who just rescued you from a most untenable position." Edward shook his head, his eyes dark with concern.

Betsy bit her lip and lowered her gaze. She was in the wrong and she well knew it. What must Edward think of her after his rescue? Why, it was worthy of one of Mrs. Radcliff's heroes. A smile touched her lips, but she forced it back.

The expression of horror on Edward's face brought shame at her behavior. Her heart sank at his low, "If I had not come… Oh, Betsy…" He did not need to paint the picture any more clearly.

Betsy closed her eyes as she again smelled the liquor and felt the man's arms about her. Shuddering, she forced away the image to focus on her reasons for going to the mission. She said no one was available to go to the mission with her, but had not Baron Fritton volunteered? Betsy frowned. Strange. She had not even remembered his offer at the time. That bore some consideration, but not here or now, not when Edward, still frowning, awaited a response.

Sucking in a deep breath, Betsy faced Edward. If there was an awkward moment, this was it. It was hardly the impression she'd hoped to make when he returned and she met him for the first time again after so many years. "I know and I am sorry. I did not use good judgment, I'll allow that."

She tucked the edges of her skirt under her legs as she tried to make herself look less like a mindless peagoose. "Understand, we help down at the mission all the time."

"Not just you, though."

Betsy shook her head as she worried her lip. "Never before just me. Spensor will be all out of countenance when he hears."

"I should think so." Edward steadied the horse that again shook its head, jingling the hardness. "So, what possessed you to do such a noddycock thing?"

Betsy felt her anger rise again, but forced herself to civility. After all, he did have a point, several really. By now she wished she'd stayed home or thought of Baron Fritton. "Everyone else in the house had plans. I remembered, too late, an appointment at the mission."

"Surely, someone could have accompanied you." Edward's tone softened. "Betsy, you are much too lovely a woman to be unescorted even in safer areas of London. But down here?"

Betsy flushed with humiliation and pleasure. Edward thought her lovely? *Oh my!*

Her reasons sounded less and less sound. "The people in the neighborhood know me. I thought…I thought I'd be all right the few steps from the cab to the door."

"Obviously not. Did not work out so well, did it?" It was not a question. Lowering her gaze, Betsy stared at her clutched hand, wishing she was any place but here.

"I did not realize. I mean, men like that. How could they… Oh my." Betsy stuttered, unable to articulate further the horror of realization as she glanced up again. She knew Edward read it all in her face.

He sucked in a breath and glanced away. "Oh, Betsy, pretty women like you are always in danger from his sort."

Pretty. Edward Denning called her *lovely* and now *pretty.* No one had ever called her either one, not with her rather long face and small nose that didn't seem to quite fit her face. *Pretty? Lovely!* Did he truly see her that way? Only the marquis seemed to share his opinion. Did they not see? Still and all, the compliment silenced her, but only momentarily. "He was foxed."

"I am convinced of it. Nevertheless, men like him have an eye for comely women." Edward winced. "Unfortunately, his state made him unable or unwilling to realize the obvious."

Betsy shook her head. "Obvious what?"

Edward let a smile lift his lips momentarily. Did she see a hint of longing in those blue eyes? *Oh dear.* She'd be heading to bedlam next if she did not take care. Botheration! The man was a missionary, not a peer hanging out for a wife. She repeated, "What's so obvious?"

"That you are obviously a woman of quality. Though I wonder why he was near the mission."

"The mission." Betsy sat up, her eyes wide. "The mission. Oh dear!"

Edward glanced at her. "The mission, what about the mission?" A moment later, he slapped his forehead. "The mission." They stared at each other.

Betsy broke the silence. "You were headed to the mission? Why?"

"To preach."

"Oh my." Betsy wiped a bead of sweat from her forehead. "I was to be there to introduce the preacher sent to the mission." Her laugh was weak at best.

Edward eyebrows rose as he glanced at her. His cheek twitched. "Is it too late?"

Betsy glanced at the watch hanging from her neck as a necklace. The chased gold exterior shimmered in the sunlight. "There is still time. I came early…as did you."

"Praise the Lord for that. I am not used to London any longer and hoped to speak to the person in charge before the service."

Betsy tried to quell a grin. "It appears you have done so."

This time Edward shook his head. "So it appears. Though I do wish that individual took fewer chances with her person—even on my behalf."

"To own the truth—" Betsy wiped her forehead before continuing "—I have had quite enough excitement for the day."

"As for excitement…" Edward stared around at his

surroundings. "I do fear I am hopelessly lost. Miss Carrington, would you be able to point me in the proper direction? I think the gray here has had enough time to rest and is as anxious to be off as you and me."

Betsy also took in the surroundings, her gaze narrow as she assessed their direction. "That's it. I know where we're at." She motioned the turns as they headed out. "There. Turn there."

Edward followed her directions and before long they arrived back at the mission. She gulped as he lifted her from the rig and offered his arm. She glanced about for the would-be kidnapper and sighed with relief when the neighborhood remained amazingly quiet. Even the dogs that usually prowled about must have found better pickings elsewhere or been asleep.

"Come. Let me introduce you inside."

Later she'd figure out what to do about getting home undetected.

Sitting in the abbreviated service after her ordeal, Betsy was mesmerized by the confident presence of the Reverend Edward Denning. Her heartbeat quickened every time he glanced her way, for when he did, he seemed to lose his place. Betsy had to remind herself Angella's brother was a pastor, a minister, whose heart beat for sharing the gospel.

Who was she? The no-account daughter of a minor peer. Even if Edward complimented her looks, she knew the truth about herself, though her recent successes forced some reevaluation and growth in confidence. Still and all, she was hardly top drawer.

Betsy shook her head. Why ever was she even considering the man who seemed to grow in stature as he paced across the small platform? There were some well-intentioned ministers who agreed to speak, but who had no idea how to reach those who had already lost their last hope—if they ever had any.

Edward was certainly of a different stamp, and it warmed her heart. Glancing around, Betsy watched a young woman in a gown that was scarcely decent, leaning forward, while a young boy in a tattered coat listened without shifting, giggling or laughing. Reverend Denning spoke directly to their needs and seemed to understand their backgrounds as she never truly had. A blush touched her cheeks. As much as she tried to reach out, from watching and listening to Edward, Betsy realized how far she'd come short in actually understanding or in reaching hearts.

These were real people with real needs, needs that were not addressed simply with money or another change of clothes. Why had she not comprehended this before? She felt tears sting her eyes and wiped them away. How much more she could have done. How much more she could have given.

She almost felt as though the words were as much for her as for the dregs of lost humanity who sat on the hard benches. Edward stepped down from the high platform and talked directly to those in the pews. He took a hand here, gave a hug there. The smell did not appear to bother him, nor the grime on faces and clothes.

Even in the clean building the odor of unwashed bodies overpowered. Unlike Edward, Betsy shrank from the smell—always had. She gave smiles, an encouraging word, clothing and household goods—and lots of good intentions. Was it all simply good intentions? Shame settled inside as well as a commitment to change and to see the people, not simply circumstances.

"Oh, Lord." She bowed her head. Here she was, entertaining a future with Edward, and he was so above her touch in all that mattered. She wanted to groan. Such a godly man and she came up so short. "Forgive me, Lord."

Edward could not help glancing toward Betsy from time to time. He tried not to. Every time he did, he lost his train of thought momentarily. It was lowering to realize how her presence set him in a spin. Taking himself firmly in hand, he focused on the audience. Their faces showed evidence of pain and despair. Some eyes sparked with hope, others with cynicism. These probably simply wanted a place to sit down and rest. Some wore clothes that had never seen better days. Others dressed in what he was sure were handouts. Some showed evidence of a lack of regular meals. So like India. So sad. He spoke of God's love and care to a people who probably had no idea what that even meant. It all broke his heart.

Stepping down from the platform that made him someone above their touch, he mingled with those who needed more than words. They needed caring human touch. These people needed so much and he had so little. He reached into his pocket and surreptitiously passed out what little he had.

He found tears on Betsy's face as she glanced up at him. He stuttered, wanting nothing more than to pull her into his arms. He shook his head, trying to stay focused. This was not the time or place to think of her.

And yet… He had compromised her by being alone

with her. Though, as far as he knew, no one had seen them. But who knew who might have been in the carriages and other vehicles they drove by in the street? The last thing he wished to happen was for Betsy to become the latest on dits. As he finished, another thought stopped him. Betsy was his responsibility. He knew now what he must do. He frowned. He also needed to deal further with Betsy about that matter of coming here without an escort. That must stop immediately.

After the service, Edward drew Betsy from her seat and kept her beside him as those in attendance filed out. She graciously introduced him to those who regularly attended. Her smile was infectious, eliciting return smiles.

Yes, this lady was quite a woman. Still and all…

Betsy knew her smile wobbled as Edward handed her into his worn rig. The gray stretched his head and seemed eager to be gone. Surprisingly, the animal had been left alone outside the church, even without someone watching the rig. She glanced up. Someone certainly watched out for the man. She recalled her escape not so long past. Maybe God watched out for one silly young woman, as well.

"Thanks, Lord," she murmured quietly as she settled on the seat. She held on as Edward leaped behind the gray and took up the reins.

"I trust you can lead us back to civilization?"

She nodded, wondering why her throat felt tight. The man beside her was a saint, a man of God, and she'd had thoughts that were far from spiritual about him. *Oh dear,* she thought, *I must not think of him like that.*

What would he see in her anyway, but the friend of his younger sister?

With an unsteady hand, she directed him until they made it safely back to a more familiar thoroughfare. "I must take you home, Miss Carrington."

"Betsy, please. We went over this." Why so formal? His tone brought unease to her middle.

"As you wish—Betsy." He paused a long, too-long, moment. They tooled along for a time, neither speaking. Betsy sensed Edward mulled something over and feared what he might say.

The silence overwhelmed her. "You reached their hearts."

Edward glanced at her and away. "God spoke through me. They are beloved of our Savior and no different from you or I, but for the status of their birth."

"I know, but…" Betsy did not like feeling he reprimanded her. "Other ministers are, well, too pompous by half."

Edward's lips tightened and Betsy sensed he chose to keep his uncomplimentary thoughts to himself. Betsy forged ahead. "Will you come again?"

This time, Edward caught her eye. "I have to think on that. Depends on my other obligations before I return to India."

She had wondered about his future and hoped he'd make a home with Angella. Now she realized her hopes were nothing more than fantasy. Her heart sank. "You are not staying in England?"

"I cannot. God called me to India." He sighed. "The need is so great." He steered the gray over to the left to avoid a cabriolet being tooled far too fast for the road and traffic conditions. Thinking she recognized the personages in the other vehicle, Betsy averted her head until they passed by.

She almost missed his next words. "I have business to handle here first." After a long moment, Edward said, "I might consider preaching again on one condition."

"Which is?" Betsy wiped sweaty palms on her gown.

"You must promise never, ever to go to that part of town without an escort. And…" His gaze narrowed, though his lips turned up ever so slightly, as he continued. "For you that does not mean a hackney cabdriver."

Betsy hung her head. "I admit it was a rather wet-goose thing to do."

"Very havey-cavey. We explored this earlier. For all I am glad I was on hand when you needed me, I wish it had not been necessary. Had I arrived a moment or two later…"

Betsy glanced at him and away, hoping he'd drop the subject. He didn't.

"Do you promise?" So he noticed she tried to avoid the promise.

"*La,* you win." She sighed. "I promise I will not go to the mission by myself."

"Or without proper escort." Edward's expression remained firm.

Betsy parroted, "Or without proper escort."

"All right, then." Again the brief pause. Betsy sensed his relief. "Mayhap next time I might escort you and your mother."

Betsy caught her breath. "I'd like that." A smile sparkled her eyes. "I'd like that very much."

Edward's hold on the reins tightened. When she turned that smile on him with those big brown eyes…

The gray nodded his head and slowed. Realizing what he was doing, Edward let the reins slip through his fingers, giving the gray his head and the signal to keep moving. This woman was so much more than his memories, his dreams.

He sent up a prayer of thanks that she'd agreed to always have an escort. That greatly relieved his mind. He wanted to slap his forehead, though. What had possessed him to offer his services as her escort? The lady had prospects and he was sure he would not be considered among those prospects. Her parents would surely show the door to a poor missionary.

Still and all, though unintended, he had compromised her. He noted her ducked head when the cabriolet went by. That incident increased the possibility that someone of her status witnessed her driving with him—alone. Inside he groaned.

He must settle the situation between them, and the prospect left him queasy.

Chapter 8

Betsy could tell from his expression that Edward mulled something over in his mind, and she half feared what it might be. Unable to wait, and knowing the answer, Betsy asked, "Have you made contact with your sister, Angella?"

Edward's frown deepened. He glanced at her and away. The deep anger in his eyes bothered her. Angella had reason for concern about her brother.

"Not yet," was all he said, though from the tightness of his shoulders and the death grip on the reins, Betsy sensed something seriously amiss. She considered telling him that he would be taking her to the very place her sister resided. In fact, she was about to speak when she started at Edward's growl.

"I shall find her soon enough, and when I do, I shall know what that cousin of yours has been about."

Betsy's gaze narrowed at the implied accusation. She straightened. "Just what might you mean by that statement? Sounds like you accuse my cousin of something havey-cavey."

"I have my reasons." Edward stared straight ahead.

"Care to share what Spensor has done to raise your ire?"

Betsy sensed his tension and gritted her teeth. Getting information out of the man set her on edge. When Edward shook his head, she asked again, "What reasons might those be?" Betsy kept her tone deliberately calm and low, though her anger rose.

She took note they had left behind the hastily, badly constructed structures and now drove by more solid dwellings of those who labored for a living as shoemakers, milliners and more. Before long, she would need to provide directions.

"Do you really know Lucashire, know his reputation?" Edward did not wait for her to reply. "I have asked about him. He has been quite the man about town, indulging in many of the less than upstanding pursuits of his peers."

Betsy knew and had no defense, except Spensor was not that man any longer—not since Angella. A small smile turned up her lips. "You refine too much on the tittle-tattle of jealous tabbies."

"Maybe so." Edward seemed to consider this. "But he took in my sister. You knew this, did you not?"

Betsy shifted in the seat. When a breeze picked up the edges of her gown, she carefully tucked it around her before answering, "Not at the time."

Edward's frown, which had eased, now deepened. "So he did take her in…and without a chaperone."

What could she say? "So I heard. But it is not as you imagine." Betsy tried to make him see beyond his fears. "Spensor is a good man."

"So you say. What man would refuse an innocent the protection of a companion or at least a chaperone? The man is a rake out to make sport of my innocent sister." Edward gulped and glared over at her. "I cannot hold that you stand up for him."

Betsy sat up. "Stop right there, Reverend Denning. That is quite enough. Spensor is not a rake, and if he partook of what his society offered, it is because he…" Betsy wasn't sure how to continue. She lived primarily in the country, where her parents had greatly sheltered her. When she did interact with her cousin, he played her gallant. She knew this other person existed, but she'd never witnessed that side of her cousin.

"See, you have no defense. I have to find Angella before the man destroys her forever. No telling what liberties he has taken."

"Fustian! Spensor would not think to do such as what you accuse him of." She so wished to tell him about Angella and Spensor, but something held her in check.

"I know how you hold him in high esteem, but the man sent off his fiancée so he could make sport of my sister."

Was not this exactly what Angella feared? *Oh dear.* "Stuff and nonsense! You have been listening to some Banbury tales for sure. He did nothing of the sort." Betsy frowned at the man beside her. What happened to the godly man who made her feel humble by comparison?

Edward frowned back. "I know you wish to think the best of your cousin and all, but…"

She would not let go. "And you, mister godly minister, are determined to think the worst of the situation when you really know nothing, nothing at all."

"I know what the vicar of Little Cambrage told me. He was most concerned."

"You have no idea!" Betsy recalled Angella's story about the "concerned" vicar. "You would rather take the word of that lascivious vicar than trust your sister? Do you have any idea what the man is like, what he did to your sister?"

Edward winced and glanced away. "I've been told some of what he did to Angella."

"If she was so brave as to be branded an evil woman and banned from the village in which she grew up rather than accept that dreadful vicar's proposal, do you believe God would send someone worse to rescue her? Why, why…" Betsy spread out her arms as she spoke. "That would be like that awful peer rescuing me from you, rather than the other way around."

"Not quite the same, but I see your point." Edward winced and pain filled his eyes. "She may not have had any choice after he took her to Lucashire Hall." He choked on the last word.

Betsy almost—almost—felt sorry for him. "Fustian! You really believe the fiddle-faddle the vicar fed you? Let me tell you—"

Edward gave her little opportunity. "Dash it all! I did not like the vicar above half. Yet what else am I to believe? Lady Margaret confirmed everything he said… and more. What she said…" Edward shook his head. "When I get hold of Lucashire, I'll discover the truth."

"Stuff and nonsense, Edward. I believe you have already made up your mind about the situation."

Edward clamped his mouth shut, then growled, "If he has harmed Angella…"

"You'll what? Come on, Edward, you'll what?" Betsy reached for his arm and found it hard with tension. "You must stop this. Lady Margaret is not the most reliable of witnesses. She was only after Spensor's deep pockets. From what I understand, he had already sought a reason to discontinue their less-than-amicable engagement."

"And you, Betsy, will not realize what is right there to see. Angella had no place to go but to Lucashire Hall, and your cousin took advantage of her."

Betsy had not realized how deeply the situation angered Edward.

His expression held fury, and the hands holding the reins were white with his grip. The gray slowed, threw up his head and jerked until Edward released his death grip.

"He did nothing to dishonor your sister." Betsy's hold on her temper faded at the insufferable stubbornness of the man she'd prayed for since she was in the schoolroom.

Her fury matched his. Hands on her hips, Betsy told him, "You presume way too much, Reverend." Betsy had about had enough of the man's assumption that her cousin was guilty of the charges leveled against him. The man she had prayed for and dreamed about for the past four years had crumbled into someone she did not know, or even want to know. She did decide she was not about to give him Angella's direction until she could warn both her and her cousin of Edward's state of mind.

"She lived with him, for months, alone. It is not done."

Betsy spoke slowly and enunciated clearly as though

speaking to a child. "Fustian! You dishonor not only my cousin, but also your sister and your faith. You act as though God was not part of this."

"Well, people make choices."

"Yes, they do, Edward, and you are making all the wrong ones."

"She was alone with him for months."

"As her guardian and with a houseful of servants. An army could live at Lucashire Hall and scarcely run into one another."

"She was alone…." She heard the forlorn note in Edward's tone.

"That, Reverend, does not mean he hurt her in any way. Things aren't always what they seem. Do not blame Lucashire for your failure to be on hand when your parents died."

This seemed to confuse Edward, and a twitch started in his cheek. "Mayhap. Yet…all that time with him…"

"True. Just what complexion would be placed on me being alone with you all afternoon, Edward? Have you taken advantage of me?"

"I rescued you!"

"Yes, you did, and for that I thank you. My cousin also rescued your sister. But someone coming along right now might come to another conclusion, might they not?"

Edward actually colored. "I did not, never would, would not think…"

Betsy jerked her jacket more firmly around her. "That's the problem, Edward, you aren't thinking. I thought you were such a man of God. But no, you hie off, making accusations you cannot prove." Betsy felt her own anger war with sympathy as she sensed guilt in Edward that he had not been near to help his sister when she most needed his help. Still, she tried to get Edward to see truth. "I believe you want my cousin to be guilty. What about mercy, grace and waiting for the truth before making judgments?" She had the audacity to poke him.

"I prayed for you all these years you've been gone. Guess those prayers were wasted."

Edward sucked in a breath. "You prayed for me?"

"I did. Every day."

"Oh." The fire seemed to seep out of him like air from the lungs of someone who got punched.

Silence descended momentarily. "I will give what you said about your cousin some thought. I will try to reserve judgment...for now."

Betsy sighed. One disaster had momentarily been averted, though she no longer trusted the man and tried to think of some way not to have him take her to Alistair House.

She was so deep in thought, she almost missed the direction of his words. "What!"

"You are right about us being out alone so long a time." He pulled the rig under a tree near a gated park and stopped. Reaching over, he took her nearest hand in his. She felt a slight tremor in his hand.

Edward cleared his throat, coughed and again cleared his throat. "Betsy Carrington, will you do me the honor of becoming my wife?"

Joy leaped inside for a flash until reality set in. "What are you saying?" Betsy surveyed Edward's face for a hint of emotion. She witnessed concern in his blue eyes and firmness at the set of his jaw. She'd watched Spensor with Angella, and Edward's expression held little in common with the way her cousin gazed at her friend. Something else was going on here, and she tensed.

While Betsy bit her lip waiting for him to speak, Edward gulped and cleared his throat one more time. "I—I should have taken you home immediately. Instead, I drove you back to the mission and have spent most of the afternoon with you unchaperoned."

"Fustian! Nothing untoward happened." Betsy found herself getting downright impatient with the man she had held in deep affection for so long. "Poppycock. No one is going to think I'm beyond the pale for spending time riding with a minister of the gospel, a missionary. It is done, you realize."

"Not this long and not without others around." Edward's cheek twitched. "I fear my desire to complete my mission, and, and…" He hesitated before plunging on. "To spend time with a lovely young woman from my past quite overset my better judgment."

Again the compliment on her looks. If he continued in that vein, he might well turn her head. She found it difficult to stay at sword points with the man who viewed her in such a fashion. "Stuff and nonsense, Edward, why the proposal? Take me home. No will be the wiser for my little adventure."

Edward hesitated, again, and Betsy wished he'd hurry up and say what was obviously on his mind. She sighed as he continued. "Even so, I have no wish to besmirch your reputation. Not in any way. Who knows who might have seen us out together, heading into an area no gentleman would take a gently bred lady?" His sigh stirred her anger as he continued. "I see no option but that we marry. I do not have much, but…"

Betsy stared at him, forcing back the tears tickling her eyes. Her dearest dream had just become a nightmare. "Have done, Reverend Edward Denning. Stop right now. I am quite—quite out of count…conten… ance with—with you." She meant to be harsh. Instead, she felt the tears she tried to hold back slide down her cheeks.

Edward had no idea how to go on. He felt helpless in the face of Betsy's tears. Part of him wanted to run as far and fast as he could away from the situation. Another part of him wished to put an arm about her and hold her close. His indecision kept him frozen in place. He witnessed the sadness, confusion and worse—the crumbling of her respect for him. It stabbed like pain inside. He swallowed, gulped and stared at the woman who had warmed his heart and held sway in his dreams for so long.

Everything she said filtered through his mind as he sat unable to move. Betsy's defense of her cousin gave him food for thought, though he felt she refined too much of what she knew of Spensor. Surely the vicar, even if he did not care overmuch for the man, had legitimate concerns. As for Lady Margaret… Her manner did leave him uneasy. Still and all, she had called off the engagement and that had to mean something havey-cavey must have been going on. Helpless, hopeless anger still burned inside, though Betsy's words had an effect—more than she might realize.

As Betsy herself pointed out, the afternoon alone with her reminded him his actions were not above reproach. He thought about his ministry in India and how he'd desired someone to walk alongside him. Someone to hold him when needs of the people overwhelmed. Someone who understood and would be waiting for him when he returned from his travels into the interior.

While a mate could travel with him most of the time, some of those missions were dangerous and he went alone or with another missionary who understood the hardships and danger.

Yes, he prayed for God's guidance on a mate and dreamed of Betsy, but he realized his finances would go from tight to impossible for two. Had he not given that desire to the Lord—many times? He sucked in a breath. One glance at the woman beside him and his heartbeat quickened. She was everything a man could want and she cared for the very type of people to whom he felt called. She cared, had a gentle heart and he broke it. It was not to be borne.

He had asked for her hand out of duty, but had not returned to England, to London, to seek a wife. His own actions, however originally noble, thrust him into a less than desirable position. As a gentleman, he knew Betsy, however independent, deserved the best—and he was not it. He could not offer her the place in society to which she was born. But this afternoon had compromised her and her position in society should anyone learn of her whereabouts during the afternoon. Obviously his proposal left much to be desired. Not what he should have done, would have done had circumstances been different.

His ire rose. It had been a ninnyhammered thing to do to go to the mission alone. Fear followed as he considered what might have happened. Furthermore, his actions as well as those of the done-up peer also compromised the comely woman beside him. Whether ready or not, he had tried to rectify the situation with his proposal. He had made her cry, and that made him feel helpless.

The anger and hurt of her response to his proposal set him back. Betsy's expression held sadness as she gazed at him. The tears on her cheeks scared him. "Betsy, what did I do wrong? Why are you crying? Please, dear, I do not understand."

Finally he tried to put an arm around her, but she pushed him away. He found his confusion etched on her face, as well. Mayhap he had not been formal enough. After all, Betsy was a lady.

"Miss Elizabeth Carrington, may I please have your hand in marriage?"

The tears continued as Betsy shook her head as she swiped at the tears.

"Please talk to me. I don't understand." Of course, she *was* a lady and probably had other offers. It was lowering to realize, while they might have areas of agreement, she was still very much above his touch. Was that it?

"Betsy. Betsy. I did not mean to insult you." Edward wiped damp hands on his jacket. "I know you are above my touch and all, but…this afternoon…" He knew he was babbling, but her silence was more than he could bear. "All alone together this afternoon. Bad part of town. Bad pass. Not done. Don't want you to suffer." Her silent tears caused him to stop for a moment, to gather his thoughts.

Lord, please help me here. Edward felt like crying, as well. He touched her arm. "Betsy, please hear me. As a gentleman, I have the duty and privilege to offer for you. I know I am not what you hoped for—"

Betsy grabbed his arm. "Stop it. Just stop it, Edward."

He felt his mouth gape in surprise when she said, "I am not above your touch."

Now he was totally confused. "But the tears?"

"Oh, Edward." He watched Betsy make an effort to calm herself. She wiped her eyes with the cambric square she pulled from the reticule that had managed to stay on her arm throughout the whole ordeal. "I will not, cannot marry you."

"But…I can speak to your father, if you like?" He'd never done this before and did not know how to go on. "Is there someone else, mayhap?"

Did he sound hopeful? Fustian! This time Betsy was firm. "No one else has claimed my hand…as yet." She recognized his confusion and his hesitation at the difference he believed between their stations in life.

"Oh, Edward, be honest. You do not wish to marry me. The only reason you offered for me was this afternoon. You are, as you say, simply being a gentleman."

Edward glanced away, then back, his expression difficult to read. "Betsy, you are all that is kind and good. A man would be a fool not to want you or to deliberately hurt you in any fashion. I am so sorry if I did so."

Betsy read the truth in his pained expression. "But you did not return to take a wife. You returned to see to your sister's future."

"Yes, that is true." Edward let out a breath she doubted he even realized he held.

Betsy closed her eyes for a moment. How could one's dreams turn into such a bad pass? After she learned the man of her dreams had feet of clay, he proposed out of some misplaced gallantry. Not that it was wrong to do so, but did he realize that from the desperate look on his face the very idea made him feel trapped?

"No one knows," Betsy told him firmly. "You will not speak to my mother. She would positively go into decline if she learned what almost happened this afternoon. Besides, Reverend Denning, I have no intention of marrying you. Because—because, face it, you don't want to marry."

Edward's shoulder eased and the tension on his face faded. Did the man have to look so relieved?

His next words somewhat mitigated his obvious relief. "Betsy, if I were to marry, I would be honored if it were you."

Something warmed within her. Mayhap she was not a total antidote.

He took up the reins. "This makes it all worse. I must get you home straightaway. Please, give me your direction and we'll be on our way."

Betsy considered what to do. She must not take him to Alistair House. His irrational anger made him less than reasonable of his sister's situation. There was time enough for him to discover the truth about his sister and Spensor. The last thing she needed after this trying day was for Edward to make a cake of himself with his accusations should she allow him to escort her home.

The solution presented itself. With a tight smile, she gave him the address. She sat straight as he tooled the rig down the wide street. Straw spread on the roadway muted the sound of the gray's hoofbeats. Betsy breathed a prayer as Edward pulled up in front of an imposing Gothic-style edifice.

"You are staying here?" From his tone, she knew

he felt intimated and probably more than ever regretted his offer.

She tried to reassure him without actually telling a whisker. "It is not ours. This season we are guests of the owner of the place in which we're staying." There, not a lie, but Edward appeared less tense.

He prepared to get down. "Here, let me see you in."

Betsy pushed him back and managed to get down on her own. "No, please. Better no one know about this afternoon."

"But—"

"I am fine. It is but a few steps to the front door. Now go...."

"Might I see you again?" Edward pulled the reins slightly as the gray shook his head.

"Mayhap...I don't know." She had to get him on his way before someone saw her.

Though his expression remained troubled, Edward nonetheless did her bidding and flipped the reins. Betsy watched until he turned the corner. She waved until he was out of sight.

Quickly, she lifted her gown, hurried across the street, cut through a backyard to the next street and, after straightening her gown, hat and jacket, she smiled and walked into Alistair House.

Chapter 9

Meanwhile, Betsy sighed with relief when she managed to evade members of the household until she was just outside the door of her bedchamber. She turned as Angella exited her room. "Why, Betsy. Haven't seen you all day. Where did you hie off to?"

Unable to hide the flush in her cheeks, Betsy turned away so Angella wouldn't see the guilty expression on her face. Too late. Taking her arm, Angella stared into her face. "Um. Something untoward happened to you." Her expression held concern. "Are you all right? Mayhap I should get Sponsor…"

"No. No, absolutely not. You mustn't." Opening her door, Betsy pulled Angella inside and closed the door.

Shaking free of Betsy's grip, Angella stuck her hands on her hips. "Just where have you been, Betsy? Your gown is stained, your stocking torn and your hair is mussed. Yet, as far I know, you have not been out with either your mother or Lady Alistair."

When Betsy struggled to know what to say or whether to confide in Angella, her friend guessed. "You have been out. Do not tell me you went out unescorted? Really, Betsy, even I wouldn't do such a noddycocked thing in London." Angella was not going to let this go and Betsy knew that, especially when her friend sat down in a chair by the hearth, crossed her arms…and waited. "Well, out with it."

"Oh, all right." Betsy put down her reticule and sat in a chair opposite her friend. "Where to start?"

Angella sent her a wry glance. "How about at the beginning?" She grinned. "I have a feeling you've had quite the adventure."

"Too much." Betsy pulled the pins from her hair and came away with a twig and leaf or two. As she combed her fingers through her disheveled hair, Angella raised her eyebrows. "Just where did you hie off to this afternoon?" She leaned forward. "And with whom."

Color flooded Betsy's cheek, which raised a question in Angella's eyes. "Surely you didn't go off with the marquis?" When Betsy shook her head, Angella asked, "Not the baron."

"No, neither."

Angella returned to her earlier guess. "Alone?"

Betsy reluctantly nodded. Angella's eyes widened. "Oh my. Are you truly all right?"

Taking a deep breath, Betsy told her, "I got word one of our sponsors was sending out someone to preach at the mission."

"You did not say anything." Angella's eyes darkened with suspicion.

"Botheration! Everyone was either gone or had plans. What was I going to do?" Betsy shrugged.

"You might have sent back a message to explain the circumstances."

Betsy grimaced. "I did not think of that."

Angella frowned. "Did not you say Fritton offered to escort you?"

"He did."

Angella finished her thought. "But you forgot about him, as well."

Betsy sighed and fidgeted. If Angella responded in such a fashion, she surely did not want her mother to know anything about her afternoon.

"So you really did go alone, didn't you?" When Betsy nodded, Angella shook her head. "Oh, Betsy. How did you get there?"

"Hackney cab."

She wilted under Angella's horrified "Oh, Betsy, havey-cavey thing to do."

Betsy raised her hands. "We're known in the neighborhood. I thought—"

"I take it things did not go as planned."

"You might say that. I was almost to the door when…" Though they were in Betsy's room, she lowered her voice and leaned over as she told her friend about the rakeshame who tried to abduct her.

"Truly, he thought you were a doxy?" Her friend covered her mouth. "Spensor will read you a scold when he hears."

Betsy clutched Angella's arm. "Please, you must not tell him. Nothing happened. Please promise."

"Nothing happened?" From her expression, Betsy

knew her friend hesitated, and she pressed her advantage. "He tried to drag me to his carriage, but…"

"You are too brave, Betsy, but very foolhardy. Why, you could have been taken away and assaulted."

Betsy was unable to hide her expression, drawing a gasp from her friend.

"Were you set upon…assaulted in any fashion at all?"

"I tried to explain, but the nob was pretty done up and not quite in his right mind." Betsy blushed to her hair roots as she continued. "He could not be persuaded I was not a woman of that stamp."

"Oh my. Betsy, what did you do? How did you get away?"

Betsy shook her head as a tiny smile lifted her lips. "You'll never believe what happened."

Betsy exploded her tidbit. "Edward rescued me."

Shock slackened Angella's expression. "Edward, as in my brother?"

"The same. There I was, fighting to get away, and Edward tooled his rig right up next to us and literally yanked me into the rig beside him."

"You're sure it was my brother, Edward?"

"Not at that moment. In that moment I felt relief followed by terror that something worse was happening." She grinned. "He soon put my fears to rest." Color stole into her cheeks. "He recognized me first."

"You are absolutely sure it was Edward?"

"Really, Angella, I do know your brother. Even without an introduction—though he is much changed."

Wonder sounded in Angella's tone. "Then Edward is in London."

"Quite so. That is how he came to be on hand to

rescue me. He was scheduled to speak at the mission. Though I did not know it, he was the very reason I felt compelled to go to the mission—to introduce whoever was sent to preach." Betsy paused, remembering. "They sent Edward and he preached a fine sermon. Fit right in at the mission."

After Angella absorbed the information, her gaze narrowed and Betsy realized her friend had noted the peculiar expression on her face before she could wipe away all the feelings evoked during the afternoon. "Betsy, there is much more to this story. Now, out with it."

She did not need much coaxing. Angella already knew the highlights. Betsy filled in the rest.

Angella shook her head. "The chances you took. But Edward knows our direction now. Sounds like he's angry enough to do something foolish. He was always my protector. I hate to think what mischief he'll cause, before he accepts the truth of the matter."

"If only Spensor had not been so caper-witted as to not send for a chaperone immediately on your arrival."

This time Angella blushed. "Afraid becoming a guardian so unexpectedly quite put him in a spin. We wrangled about everything. Then—then things changed when he returned to his faith."

"Which he credits to you." Betsy smiled.

"Then he found a chaperone, but it was too late. The village tabbies preferred a tale of scandal."

"Which your brother has swallowed whole."

"Now that he knows where I am, he'll return."

"He won't." Betsy shrugged. "As to our direction—dash it all, I could not abide his insinuations. So he doesn't know. I told him to let me off at that large house over a street. I felt you needed time to prepare for any visit. He might consider what I said, or not, but I could tell anger burned within and he was not ready to hear another explanation." She sighed. "Sorry."

Angella reached forward and patted Betsy's arm. "You did the right thing. Mayhap if Spensor and I go to him…"

"Oh dear!" Betsy clapped a hand to her mouth. "I was so caught up in not letting him know your direction, I neglected to discover where he is staying. Oh, I am so sorry."

"He won't stop looking for me—especially now that he has found you again." A slight smile tugged at Angella's lips as she changed the subject. "He actually asked for your hand?"

"He did, but…he seemed all too relieved when I turned him down. How lowering."

"Betsy, I think you refine too much over that. Be glad Edward came to your rescue. Mayhap you'll write adventure romance stories one of these days."

Betsy rolled her eyes. "Mine would be about silly chits making bad choices and being rescued by handsome missionaries. Not a story most want to read. I am convinced God put Edward there at that moment." Silence reigned for a few moments.

Reaching over, Angella squeezed Betsy's hand. "God is in this somehow. I would love having you for my forever sister."

"I would like that as well, but Edward acted so strangely over Spensor. I worry about a man with so much anger. He did not seem like the same man who spoke with such comfort and hope at the mission."

Angella glanced away and back. "Quick temper runs in the family, I fear."

"It matters not." Betsy found herself holding back a tear. "As for that proposal—dreadful. I guess I was goose-witted to hope for something more heartfelt instead of a dreaded obligation. I do not know why I expected something else." She sighed. "Truly, Edward scarcely knows who I am. We met only that one time at the reception after his commissioning service. I could not forget, but…"

"I have a feeling you haven't heard the last of my brother yet."

Betsy tried to protest, but a bell sounded. "Angella, look at me. I am not ready for dinner. What will I do? Mother cannot know about today. Sponsor either." At the skeptical look in her friend's eyes, she begged. "Please, Angella, I am fine. I promised your brother I would not do such a hen-witted thing again. And I won't. Now please."

Angella stood and straightened the skirt of her gown. "Be thankful we're dining in tonight. Get ready, but hurry. I'll see about delaying things a bit." With that, she left Betsy to dress, without aid of a maid, and ponder the afternoon. Was Angella right? Was there hope?

After leaving off Betsy, Edward frowned as he tooled the gray down the road. Unease sat on his shoulders at not seeing Betsy into the house. What a rag-mannered thing to do! He should not have listened to her, even if she was a tad put out with him over his proposal. More than a tad. He still did not quite understand her overreaction. Still, he was a gentleman. Turning the gray, he found his way back to the house. Betsy was nowhere about. What did he expect, that she would wait for him? Shaking his head, Edward sent up a prayer as he headed back to the home of Reverend Jeremiah.

"Well, Lord, I made a grand disaster of this afternoon. Betsy probably now thinks I am a loose screw. But what else could I have done but offer?" He sighed, feeling as though his sister's situation and his relationship with Betsy placed a heavy weight on his shoulders. Somehow he must make things right.

"I really must see her again, Lord." Why? To explain? How, when he had not done such a bang-up job the first time around. He did not look too deeply into why he felt the need to contact Betsy again. "She is top drawer, Lord. Is there hope or am I fooling myself and exchanging the heavenly for the earthly?" Did he have the courage to speak on the subject to his mentor? It bore some thought.

Edward was less than enthusiastic about attending the dinner party that evening. Reverend Jeremiah, as usual, had invited others over for dinner and expected Edward at the table. Edward stilled a sigh as he sat beside a tall, thin pastor determined to change the political landscape and a short, wide minister who applied himself to the bountiful repast with only a grunt or two to show he listened to the conversation around him.

While Reverend Jeremiah lived frugally, he insisted on a cook who knew what he was about. An invitation to one of the minister's dinners was seldom turned down. Guests accepted even knowing the minister extended invitations with a purpose he revealed after the meal.

The home of Edward's mentor had been inherited from a well-to-do grandmother and was in a decent enough part of town. Though he seldom spoke of his family, Edward knew Jeremiah's elder brother held a title. The minister often housed other ministers traveling through the area and provided inexpensive housing for students planning to enter the ministry, which was how Edward originally came in contact with the man. Two wide-eyed students listened to the spirited discourse around them.

Was he once so young, so naive? Those times felt so long ago. One minister was not of the area, but others, Edward either recognized or had heard about. After his day, he wished only for his chambers to contemplate the afternoon and what he might have done differently. Thinking back, he realized how upset Betsy became at his accusations against her cousin and how little real information she provided him. He straightened. Betsy knew where his cousin was and probably his sister, as well.

He gulped back a groan. His overriding anger closed off his primary source of information. But there was more and he really needed someone's advice. Reverend Jeremiah had once had a wife. She'd been as kind as he. She died of pneumonia while he was away. Nonetheless, the man had been married for nigh on twenty years or more. Surely, Reverend Jeremiah understood the female mind—at least more than he did himself.

Earlier, on the way back to his quarters, Edward realized his need to ask for counsel and had been rather Friday-faced as he dressed for dinner. Mayhap after the prolonged meal and after the guests returned home, the minister would have a moment for him. It was not to be. Not that night. The minister had other things on his mind.

For a long time after retiring to his room, Edward read his well-worn, leather-covered Bible. To the horror of some, he had taken to actually writing notes in the book. God spoke. Edward listened and wrote out His insights. His Bible was now like an old friend, but that night it did not speak to him as he hoped. He even tried setting the Bible spine down and letting the book fall open, but it always opened to his favorite passages. The problem was he knew the Word, knew where to find scripture to shore up his point of view. Was he not being righteous in his attitude toward the earl?

He shifted uncomfortably, recalling Betsy's accusations. He recalled, too, his mentor's admonition to wait, pray and make certain of the truth. Yet deep inside, fury built. He knew young men of a certain station thought nothing of accosting and using those they believed beneath them.

Groaning, he let his head drop into his arms. "Lord, please. This is burning me up inside. It is so hard to let this anger go. I need to discover the truth of the matter."

He paused. Even in his anguish, Betsy's face brought a slight smile. Yet her disgust of him pained him deep inside. He had made it so much worse with that proposal. How he must have hurt her tender sensibilities with his less-than-enthusiastic offer.

He all but heard his words played back in his mind and cringed. A lovely lady like his Betsy deserved so much more. His Betsy? He had no right to call her his, but, oh, he realized with sudden clarity he wanted to do so. How he truly wanted her to be his Betsy.

He tried so hard to keep his mind away from thoughts of hearth, wife and family. Betsy brought all those desires back with force. "Lord, is she a temptation or are you trying to tell me something?"

He said as much when he caught his mentor a couple of mornings later.

Reverend Jeremiah rubbed his clean-shaven face. "You have feelings for the girl?"

Misery crowded out words and Edward merely nodded. His tongue loosed and he rattled, "She is all that is lovely and kind and good and…"

He noted the almost smile on the face of his mentor. "But I bungled things so badly. Besides, how can I ask someone so fine to join me in India? I know I must forget about her—"

His mentor interrupted. "Why? Does she not care about the needs of the poor and needy?"

"Well, yes, but—"

"Is she some silly creature interested only in her looks and the latest fashion?"

"It would not appear so, no." Edward wondered where the minister was guiding the conversation, for he was convinced the man led to a point.

"Are you God to arbitrarily decide you will not suit?"

Edward straightened. "Are you saying…?"

"I am saying that you must seek God's direction and make decisions with His leading and truth, not on your feelings or some sense of sacrifice that may not be warranted."

Edward was hard put not to let his mouth drop open. He knew the hope growing inside was mirrored on his face. His mentor made him think. Picking up his heavy Bible that looked as worn as the one Edward's father used, the minister slowly read, "Psalm 145:8, 'The Lord is gracious, and full of compassion; slow to anger, and of great mercy.'"

He flipped toward the end of the Bible. "James 1:19-20, 'Wherefore, my beloved brethren, let every man be swift to hear, slow to speak, slow to wrath. For the wrath of man worketh not the righteousness of God.'"

He ended with "Proverbs 16:32, 'He that is slow to anger is better than the mighty; and he that ruleth his spirit than he that taketh a city.'"

Edward gulped as his mentor caught his eye, his expression caring but firm. "The core of your problem isn't Betsy Carrington or your sister's situation. It is the anger toward the earl you refuse to let go of. Why don't you believe the lady? Would she lie to you?"

"No, never. Not purposely. But she may wish to believe only the best about her cousin, and—"

"Edward, son—for you are the son we never had— you almost seem to relish the idea of guilt. Why is that? What if he treated your sister with respect?"

"And if he did not?"

"Then you help your sister deal with it with grace."

Edward tried to speak, could not. His mentor got up, squeezed his shoulder and said as he departed, "You need to see this young lady again. I think she's the key to unraveling the tangle of your heart and your future. But see to that anger."

Edward caught his breath. Yes. Yes indeed—at least to seeing Betsy again.

Chapter 10

"Are you sure you will not go with us this afternoon?" Betsy looked at Angella as she faced the mirror. Betsy's maid finished pulling up her hair and handed her the spring-green hat with a saucy brim. Betsy added a short paisley cape that complemented the green of her lightweight gown. She checked herself once more in the mirror before turning to her friend and repeating her question.

Angella shook her head. "Lady Alistair is determined to go over wedding plans. I'm surprised your mother decided on this shopping trip instead of joining us."

Amusement danced on Betsy's lips. "Perish the thought of my speaking out of turn, but polite though they are, those two are working more in competition than together."

Angella grimaced. "Am I daft to wish only for a small ceremony with close family and friends?"

Betsy walked with Angella on the way downstairs. "Not at all. But there is the consequence of the Alistairs and my cousin to consider. Though—" Betsy lowered her voice "—I don't think he cares a fig for all the nonsense, either, but we are in London and he knows…"

Angella's forehead wrinkled as she walked with her friend into the drawing room, where Lady Carrington awaited her daughter.

Betsy leaned in closed and whispered, "He is doing it for your sake—your consequence. A grand wedding will have everyone looking with favor on the match—especially if they are invited."

"Oh my!" Angella's eyes widened and her hand covered her mouth. "I had no idea."

At that moment, Winter entered the room. Her long sky-blue gown whispered as she moved. The countess nodded toward Betsy's mother and smiled at Betsy before turning her attention toward Angella. "Come, my dear. We have much still to do. Besides, the dressmaker is also coming this afternoon for a fitting."

With a shrug toward Betsy and a grin, Angella left with Lady Alistair.

Not but a few minutes later, Betsy and her mother were handed into a small carriage. In front, the coachman, high on his perch, drove the perfectly matched bays. Betsy noted that, as usual, neither of the horses had its head restricted with the cruel bearing rein.

She'd commented on their absence once and was gratified when Winter, the horsewoman coming to the fore, shuddered. "What some go through to show off, not caring at all about their horses' comfort, their ability to move and breathe. Such instruments of torture should be outlawed." She paused and threw Betsy a grin. "As a horsewoman you know what I mean. I have pestered Alistair to take up the matter in the House of Lords, but so far no one else is willing to take up the cause. Instead, though you might have missed it, I wrote anonymously to *The Political Register* about the issue."

"You didn't!" At her nod, Betsy shook her head. "I heard about that piece. Put many society ladies up in the boughs. They went into a regular spin over the issue. Not sure anything came of it, though."

Winter smiled. "Ah, but a couple of my friends realized the truth and have at least loosened the bearing rein on their cattle."

All this flashed through Betsy's mind as the coachman tooled down the roadway to the mercantile establishments where they went to shop. Betsy and her mother intended to search out gowns for the wedding as well as gowns for the parties and routs that were already being planned before the big event. There were also shoes, shawls and hats. Though Betsy worried about the expense, the womanly side of her reveled in looking her best. Her thoughts turned inward, Betsy almost missed the familiar figure walking alongside the roadway.

She hoped her mother did not notice the flush in her cheeks. Simply watching him warmed her heart. As she turned her head as they drove by, Edward turned his head as well and caught her eye. Betsy sucked in a breath as she turned away and quickly fanned her burning cheeks. What nonsense!

She avoided her mother's glance of concern and readily accepted the hand of the coachman as he handed her down in front of the dressmaker's shop. Betsy contented herself with the many fabrics available from the usual muslin to colorful silks, painted cotton and satin. She checked over the various trims from cashmere, buttons and fur to intricate lace, ribbons and embroidery. Lost in choosing patterns, fabrics and trims, Betsy all but forgot the time as she and her mother ordered more gowns and accessories for the coming social engagements. Betsy was woman enough to concede the patterns and materials chosen enhanced her figure and coloring. Their purchases they ordered to be sent directly to Alistair House.

Her attention diverted to shopping, Betsy straightened, startled when she and her mother exited the dressmaker's shop only to find Edward bowing toward them. "Lady Carrington." He spoke to her mother, then hesitated as though he kept himself from addressing Betsy in too familiar a way in the presence of her mother.

Betsy stepped in. "Reverend Denning, what brings you into the district this afternoon?"

Her mother frowned, recovered. "Denning? Reverend Denning?"

Betsy knew she tried to place the name. She willed her cheeks not to color as she explained, "Mother, this is Edward…Angella's brother."

Lady Carrington became all solicitation. "It has been an age, young man. Your sister has been at sword points waiting for your arrival."

She would have continued, but Betsy interrupted. She must keep her mother from revealing too much.

Edward nodded. "Since I am in this vicinity, may I be so bold as to ask you lovely ladies to join me for an ice and sweetmeats?"

Betsy was not sure whether to laugh or cry. She had

no idea if Edward had discovered his sister's where-abouts or if he would cause a problem if he did. Until she knew…

Her mother took the decision out of her control. Fanning herself, Lady Carrington told him, "I must admit to being parched. I accept your invitation with pleasure. I'd like to know more about your ministry, young man—Reverend Denning." With that she took his proferred arm. Seeing nothing to be gained by stalling, Betsy took his other arm and sent up a prayer for wisdom and strength.

Edward sent up his own prayer, only his was a thank-you that Reverend Jeremiah had sent him to pick up a pair of boots at his bootmaker's. The owner assured Edward the boots would be ready on the morrow. He blathered on that he'd been busy and help had been ill, and more. The man droned on with excuses that Edward halted with a raised hand. "I shall return tomorrow and I expect them to be finished and ready."

The owner nodded toward him and Edward stilled a smile. The owner surveyed him and figured out he was not some rich nob and could be pawned off for another day. As he left, some high-in-the-arch nobleman entered and the owner was all solicitation about the last-minute order being hard but completed. Light dawned. The nobleman's order took precedence.

Not that it mattered overmuch, but Edward greatly disliked wasting time, and a trip to the bootmaker's meant he was not out finding the whereabouts of his sister. When he glanced up and watched Betsy exiting the dressmaker's shop, the afternoon did not seem nearly so wasted. Warmth knotted inside as he escorted the ladies across the street to a shop with a sign that swung in the slight breeze advertising itself as an eating establishment. With a flourish, he led them to a table and sat them down. Betsy's smile sent his heart soaring.

Lady Carrington abruptly brought him back to earth. As they sipped their cool drinks and consumed their treats, she frowned and Edward feared she might rap his knuckles with her closed parasol. "Now, young man, why have you not been around to see your sister? She has been through so very much these past months. You have no idea." She pulled a fan from her reticule and fanned herself.

Betsy looked positively faint, and he turned his concern toward her. "Miss…Betsy…are you all right? Are you ill? Can I get you anything?"

She put a hand on her forehead. "No, no…Reverend Denning." She emphasized the name and stared pointedly until he got the message.

Oh, she did not wish her mother to know they were on familiar terms. Why ever not? A muscle in Edward's cheek twitched. Mayhap he should not have presumed to ask such fine ladies to spend time with him. Yet Betsy's mother did not take it amiss.

He wondered if Betsy witnessed his confusion from his expression. Did she think she was above his touch? She surely was, for she was a comely enough woman, but she did not appear to be embarrassed by his presence.

Did this have to do with his sister? Did not Betsy wish her mother to pursue talk of his sister? He sensed the young woman knew more than she'd told him, and he certainly did not wish her mother to say something that would keep Betsy from sharing what she knew.

Still, it puzzled Edward. Would not her mother also know the whereabouts of his sister?

He glanced from Betsy to her mother. "I miss my sister. I returned to England as soon as I received her letter, but it has taken time to arrive in London. I do plan to look her up soon."

Betsy sighed with relief when her mother said, "All right, then. Do not put it off long. Not that it signifies all that much now, except that your presence will please Angella."

Betsy's obvious relief and her mother's words only added to Edward's puzzlement.

Why did his sister not need him? Dread, like lead, dropped in his middle. Was his sister, in truth, being kept by the earl? Was that her veiled meaning? His hands clenched around his glass, and his jaw tightened. Manners dictated he not interrogate the woman, though it meant clamping down on his tongue.

Betsy took note and her gaze narrowed as though she read his thoughts. "Don't get in a taking, Edward. Angella is safe and fine and happy. Yes, of course, she would like to see you. We shall speak of that further."

"What is wrong with now?"

"Now I would like to know what brings you down to this part of town. Surely not to shop." Her tone bit with slight sarcasm and a question.

"No. No indeed." He was not about to explain he had not the blunt for a shopping excursion. Truth be told, he scarcely had the means to pay for their afternoon treat. He'd rather lost his head on seeing Betsy and simply had to prolong the contact with her. Even to using up the last coins in his pocket. He would not have those but for his mentor. He explained the reason for his outing. Betsy seemed to accept his explanation.

"I shall return tomorrow since the shop owner decided a peer's order was more pressing than that of a minister." He smiled to take the sting from his words.

Lady Carrington nodded. "Oh yes. The way of the world. Tell me about India. I have heard it is beautiful."

Edward agreed and spent some time sharing his love of the country and the beauty of the countryside. "But there is great darkness. They need God's love and grace." He did not go into details about some of dangerous and rather disgusting traditions practiced.

"Before my husband died, we considered a trip to India."

Betsy mouth gaped. "Mother, I had no idea."

Lady Carrington patted her hand. "We never got that far in our plans before…" She paused and swallowed a couple of times before continuing. "Before he had the accident that took his life."

Betsy reached out and took her hand. "I am so sorry, Mother."

"I did not know about your husband, Lady Carrington, your father, Betsy. I am so sorry for your loss." Edward sought for some way to lighten the tension. "India is my mission and my home now. However, today I am privileged to be here spending time with two lovely ladies."

Lady Carrington smiled, accepting the compliment as her due. Betsy shook her head. More compliments? "Such flummery. I would almost think you mean it, though you are merely being polite in my case."

"What nonsense is this?"

Red spotted Betsy's cheek. "Please, Edward. I know

I'm hardy top drawer. Such flattery is not suited to a man of the cloth."

"Flattery." He felt heat on his neck. "I am not some ninnyhammered coxcomb given to speaking untruth." His anger faded at the truth in her eyes. She really did not think herself beautiful. The realization stunned him.

"Miss Carrington, you are all that is fine and lovely in a woman." The words tripped off his tongue without recall and left him embarrassed and horrified that he had so spoken his heart.

Betsy blinked and seemed bereft of words. A small smile, however, played at the corners of Lady Carrington's lips. "So that is the way of things, is it?"

Edward's heart sank when she continued. "Who is going to explain how you seem to know each other so well?"

He and Betsy stared at each other. She gulped. "Oh, Mother!"

Betsy turned her horrified gaze toward Edward. Her stomach clenched and the sweetmeat dropped like lead inside. She saw no way out of this dilemma—one she had brought upon herself. How could she ever explain? Edward understood her plea. A small smile played about his mobile lips. His blue eyes blinked, and the look he bestowed was meant to calm, or so she assumed. As he began his story in his deep pastoral tones that so moved her during his sermon at the mission, Betsy slumped into her chair.

Her mother noticed. "Dear, please sit up straight. That is no way to sit in public." She smiled at Edward. "Please go on. You found my daughter where?"

Betsy admired the way her rescuer told the story. He

sanitized it as much as possible and took as much blame
as he could—bless him. Still, as he spoke, her mother's
fan moved more and more quickly as her mother tried
to ease the heat rising in her cheeks. "Oh my," she said
more than once.

Edward ended. "So I brought her safely back home."
He took a deep breath. "I offer my most humble apologies for not returning her home immediately."

Lady Carrington impaled Betsy with a stare that
shriveled her insides. "Mother, I—"

"Going off like some silly wet goose. It is not done."
She continued to fan herself. "Oh, Betsy, what might
have happened. I cannot fathom your actions. I am quite
out of countenance with you."

Betsy gulped and wiped her damp palms on her skirt.
Thankfully, her mother turned her intensity on to Edward, who shifted under her gaze. He glanced at her and
Betsy all but choked. Surely he would not try to offer for
her now. She gave a slight shake to her head. If he had
planned such a noddycock action, her response clari-
fied the action would not gain him any favors with her.

He nodded slightly to signal he understood. At least
she hoped he understood. At any rate, he did not approach the subject and, for that, Betsy breathed a sigh
of relief. No matter what she thought about Edward—
and there was no doubt he made her heart beat more
quickly—or any other eligible *parti,* she wanted a man
to ask for her hand because he was over the moon in
love with her. Not for nothing did she read Mrs. Radcliff and similar romance novels. That reading material
was her deep secret until Angella had caught her out
and joined in her less-than-literary pursuits.

They discussed them at some length. For Betsy the

hero of all the novels had Edward's face. She blushed at the thought now as both her mother and Edward turned toward her.

"Betsy. Oh, Betsy."

The horror and fear in her mother's tone brought Betsy to the realization of how much her actions hurt and frightened her mother. She clasped her mother's hand as her throat tightened. "I am so sorry, Mother. Edward, Reverend Denning, was ever the gentleman." Her glance took in the blond-haired man beside her mother, whose gaze added to her guilt.

"I apologize to you, as well, Edward, for placing you in such an awkward position."

"Betsy, I know your heart bleeds for those in need," her mother told her, "but you must not put yourself at risk. That will not do, not do at all."

Releasing her mother's hand, Betsy hung her head. "I know. But…" She glanced from Edward to her mother. "Edward made me promise and I did. I…I should have waited, should have asked someone to go with me."

"Yes, my dear, you should have." Lady Carrington sighed, put down her fan and leaned back in her light, elegantly scrolled chair. "However, mayhap good will come of it yet."

Betsy wasn't sure she liked the glint in her mother's eyes.

"Reverend Mr. Denning, I am in your debt. You have my most humble gratitude for rescuing and protecting my daughter." She smiled at the man, who shifted uncomfortably.

"My Christian duty, milady." His words felt like an insult, and Betsy's eyes flashed.

Her words projected without thought. "Duty. Manners and all that. That's all?"

Edward actually flushed. "Ah, but...Betsy, it was my pleasure to rescue one comely young woman whom I had hoped to meet again in England."

Had he really said he had wanted to see her on this trip? This stopped her and Betsy scarcely knew what to say. Though from the withdrawn look on the man's face, he'd said more than he'd intended. Her mother caught his words as well, and a suspicious smile played on her lips.

Lady Carrington rose. "It has been...enlightening, Reverend Denning. I do give you leave to call on us soon. We shall be home except for a time in the afternoon when we plan to visit the lending library." She gave the address of the library as though hoping Edward would—what?—happen to "find" them on the morrow? Betsy tried not to roll her eyes.

Beyond the fact that her mother seemed to have set her attention on the poor man as an eligible *parti,* Betsy feared she'd hand him her calling card and then they'd be truly undone. He must not know their direction until he knew the truth about Angella and this interlude had not helped in that regard. Instead, she distracted her mother by stepping over to Edward's side and taking his arm.

So sweetly that both glanced at her with narrowed eyes, Betsy asked, "Will you be so kind as to escort us back to our carriage?"

With a neat tip of his head and a smile, Edward proffered his arms for both ladies. "My pleasure. Shall we?"

A bit later as he handed Betsy into the carriage, he

whispered for her ears alone, "I will find Angella, you know. I wish you'd help me."

She whispered back, "When you know the truth and leave behind anger."

A look she could not interpret settled in his eyes. "So you do know her direction. Trust me, Betsy, you haven't seen the last of me."

For all the misunderstanding with his sister, Betsy hoped he spoke true. She did want very much to see Edward Denning again.

Chapter 11

Later in his bedchamber, Edward paced the floor. He had bungled things again. He knew it. Being around the fetching young Miss Carrington muddled his brains. Yet again, Betsy managed to keep him from discovering more about his sister's whereabouts. At least he knew for certain Betsy was in contact with her. Really, it greatly vexed him that Angella remained so elusive. According to Lady Carrington, Angella anticipated his arrival. He frowned. That did not sound as though she was in dire straits unless—unless she hoped he would remove her from the situation. That didn't seem quite the thing, either.

"Lord, I should be more worried about Angella, and yet all I can think about is a pair of soft brown eyes that sparkle with life." Slumping into a chair that needed recovering, Edward cradled his head in his arms.

It started at the reception after his commissioning service when he had first stared into the brown eyes of Lady Carrington's daughter and could not look away. Her eyes sparked with interest as he shared his heart with her even during the short time he had with her. Why could he not forget those eyes, forget *her?*

Caught up in his mission, he realized he might well be sacrificing marriage to follow God's leading to India. How could he drag any woman of quality back to India? The thought was not to be borne, and yet, as hard as he tried—then and now—he could not forget her, did not wish to erase her from his mind and, now that he was in London, from his life.

Things were so much worse since arriving in London. He actually sought occasions to be with Betsy. When he was near the lovely, gentle Betsy, all his carefully thought out considerations fled from his mind as though erased. In truth, his mind scarce worked at all around the genteel young woman.

He felt completely torn as he wondered like a drowning man through the evening, *Lord! What am I to do?*

Ever had he scoffed at the very idea of loving on immediate acquaintance, but here he was with his heart completely and irrevocably given to this beautiful young socialite.

She was the temptation of Satan—wasn't she, to turn him from the right course as Angella had been tempted and strayed into sin? Or had she? Surely if that were true, Betsy and especially her mother would not be so accepting of the situation. These were godly women. Even for their cousin, Edward did not see them accepting an arrangement such as he had been told was the case with his only sister.

Betsy said he did not know the truth. He wiped his forehead. Even under the scorching sun of India, he'd never felt so warm. Somehow he must let Betsy go and focus on Angella. The longer the situation lasted, the longer it would take before he returned to his work in India. Truth was, Betsy held the key to finding Angella. It was a frustrating coil. He sat up. Of course! He knew where they were staying. Had he not let Betsy off at the place? He would find her and demand to know where Angella resided. Mayhap, too, he could finally get the tall, dark-haired Betsy out of his mind.

As they traveled back to Alistair House after yet more shopping, Lady Carrington surveyed her daughter. "I think you have made a conquest, my dear."

Besty groaned. "Mother. He's a minister and a missionary."

"That does not signify. Ministers need wives. In fact, they are very much in need of wives to manage their homes while they meet the spiritual needs of their congregations."

"Be that as it may, Mother, Edward, Reverend Denning, is a missionary who plans to return to India as soon as he is assured his sister is all right." Betsy wondered why she was fighting her mother on this. She should be thrilled her mother looked favorably on Edward, who had no expectations and would only marginally be accepted into their social world.

She also could not forget how much Edward had *not* wished to offer for her. That still rankled. "Why are you considering him eligible for me?"

"Because," her mother said, reaching over and tucking a stray strand of Betsy's hair back under her daughter's hat, "I see the way he makes your eyes light up."

"Oh." Betsy did not know how to respond. Unexpectedly, her eyes filled with tears. "But he doesn't wish to take a wife back to India."

Her mother smiled. "My dear, the heart has a way of making its own way. Don't give up on your young man."

"But, Mother—"

"Betsy, he's worth fighting for." Her mother leaned forward and lowered her voice. "Pray about this and follow God's guidance. He won't mislead you, my dear."

Betsy's heartbeat quickened. There was such wisdom in her mother's eyes. Was there hope? It bore some thought…and prayer.

When Betsy and her mother arrived back at Alistair House, she found Angella lying down in her bedchambers. "I am exhausted," she told Betsy. "I thought all that shopping before the season was bad, but this… Winter is very exacting and knows what she wants. She wants the dress to be exquisite, and it is, but all those fittings are driving me to distraction."

She fluffed up the large pillows and pulled herself up on the bed. "Grab a pillow and join me." As Betsy set several pillows against the head of the bed and settled down beside her friend, Angella pulled the bell cord. Not long thereafter, they shared an afternoon treat of chocolate and scones. They giggled as they tried not to get crumbs on the bed.

Betsy listened as Angella told her, in exaggerated detail, about her afternoon. "Now, tell me, how did your shopping go?"

"I found the most wonderful fabric and pattern for my gown for your wedding. Why, I might even look

passably good, though no one will see me next to you."
She paused before saying, "Guess who we ran into—
almost literally?"

"Fritton? Beddinlong?" Angella guessed a few more
names, before raising her hand in surrender. "Too many
possibilities. Give. Who was it?"

"Edward."

Angella sat up. 'You saw my brother this afternoon?"

"Indeed, and he treated us. My mother is quite taken
with him."

"That's good, isn't it?"

Besty shrugged.

"So, did you tell him?"

Betsy frowned. "Not exactly."

The next afternoon, Edward borrowed the minister's
good rig. The gray nuzzled him with almost affection
as he presented him with a piece of carrot and patted
the broad forehead and scratched his ears.

With a will, he took up the reins and, with a prayer,
he turned the eager horse toward the bootmaker's. Traffic and frisky mongrel dogs hassling the gray caused
more delay than the bootmaker, who tried to put him
off once again. In a rush to see Betsy, Edward would
have none of it. "My good man, get those boots out and
you shall have your pay immediately."

The man fairly flew into the back room, yelling orders. Edward bit back a smile. He had gone up in the
bootmaker's estimation. He well knew too many of the
upper classes were either slow to pay what they owed
or did not pay their bills at all. More than one vendor
went out of business because they had upper-class cli-
ents who thought paying their bills beneath them. It

never seemed to occur to those in society that paying their bills kept shopkeepers off the streets, in business and able to feed their families.

Such arrogance. The thoughts flitted through his mind as he waited for the bootmaker to return with the boots. Edward inspected them and found them exquisite. He wished for the blunt to have a pair made up for himself. But there was little hope of that. His boots were study enough. The bootmaker practically bowed when Edward handed him what his mentor owed.

The whole errand took much longer than planned. He breathed a sigh of relief when he left the press of animals and people behind for the stately homes where the sound of hooves was muted by layering straw on the road. He readily found the house where he had left Betsy. Hopping down, Edward secured the gray and hurried to knock at the door.

A tall butler opened the door and stared at him as though he were some lowly bug. Edward stood up straighter, swallowed. "Would Miss Betsy Carrington be in this afternoon?"

He detected a slight frown between the man's eyes. "I fear, sir, no one by that name resides at this residence."

"Are you sure?" The slight narrowing of the butler's gaze told Edward his response did not go over well. "Miss Elizabeth Carrington." Maybe her whole name would suffice.

"No one even remotely by that name resides here." Stepping back, the butler closed the door, practically in Edward's face. He stared at it momentarily.

Deuced odd. This was the place. He was sure of it. Slowly, he walked back to the gray and took up the reins. As the truth dawned, anger welled up inside. She made a fool of him, ensuring that he would not know her address. Still, she must be staying in the vicinity. He glanced around. Hopeless. He was not about to start knocking on every door.

With a sigh of defeat, he turned the gray. As he did so, he recalled Betsy's mother letting him know they planned to be at a lending library today. He recalled, too, the address. Glancing up, he hoped he was not too late. Time he and one comely young woman had a reckoning.

Betsy perused the shelves, breathing in the scent of new books with their leather covers and of old books with a slightly musty smell. She pulled down a book of history here and one of philosophy there, as well as a book of poetry. She replaced a thin volume by Lord Byron, blushing as she remembered some of what she'd heard about the man.

She had just settled onto a bench near the window to read, when a disturbance alerted her. Glancing up, she gasped as Edward stood before her. "Miss Carrington, a word if I may."

Betsy moved over and tugged the skirt of her white gown sprinkled with green, rose and yellow flowers out of his way as he sat. "I did not expect you to take Mother up on her obvious invitation."

She gulped under his steady gaze. "I don't suppose you did. And your mother?"

Betsy lifted her hand as she shrugged. "She is here— someplace."

"I went to where I left you off the other day."

Feeling his gaze on her, she flushed and stared down

at her half boots. Reaching down, she rubbed a small mud ball from the side. "I see. You went to the door?"

"I did. A rather top-lofty butler thought I had an attic to let when I asked after you." He simply watched her squirm.

His quiet interrogation irritated her. "I had my reasons, but I am sorry for your trouble."

"Are you, now?" He leaned back against the wall, his gaze still on her. She felt accused without a word.

"I will not have you upsetting your sister."

"That's the reason you continue to confound my attempts to find her whereabouts?" He made it more a statement than a question and she flushed again. What a time to notice his Spanish blue jacket showed off his shoulders to perfection. The white of his cravat—nicely tied—set off his chiseled features. Warmth having nothing to do with anger flowed through her.

"We've wrangled enough, my lady." His gaze grew more intense. "I must needs speak with my sister."

Mayhap her unwanted response dictated her waspishness. "You sister is doing well, Edward. But you don't believe that, do you?"

Edward's lips thinned. "I can hardly discern the truth of the matter when I have yet to speak with her." He paused. "I want her direction. Time for games is over. As much as I enjoy spending time with you, Betsy, my mission in London is to see to my sister's future."

"That is it?"

"Yes, it is."

Betsy blinked back tears. Oh, the man made her incredibly angry. Had he no notion how she felt, how his marked attentions did something to her heart? Were they all just to get her to reveal Angella's whereabouts?

It was not to be borne. She stood so quickly her book fell off her lap, much to her horror. Edward caught it before it hit the floor.

"Where does this go?"

She showed him and he slid it back onto the shelf. "Now, where might I find my sister?" His gaze narrowed. "Or shall I ask your mother?"

Betsy ground her teeth. "Odious man."

This brought forth a smile and increased her ire. True, he needed to see Angella, and she needed to figure it out and soon, but not here and now. Not one used to subterfuge, Betsy nonetheless took a chance. Closing her eyes, she swayed toward him. "Oh, Edward, I feel faint."

Betsy was in a taking when she arrived back at Alistair House. Angella pulled her into the parlor, away from her mother. "What is the matter, Betsy? You look positively...well, I am not sure. But something is amiss?"

"No, *everything* is amiss. Botheration! That brother of yours puts me quite out of countenance." Betsy stamped her foot.

"He does, does he?" Angella took her arm and pulled her down on the settee beside her. "Out with it. You were going to the lending library."

"So we did and your brother found us there. He was vexed that I fooled him the other day by having him let me off at a place a street away. He went there, you see."

"To see you?" Angella hid a grin behind her palm.

"*La.* That did not stop him. Guess he remembered Mother telling him where we'd be today."

"So why are you angry with my brother this time?"

Betsy tugged at her hat until it came off in her hands. She all but shredded the trailing ribbons until Angella pulled it away and set it down on the other side of her on the settee. "He was determined to find you."

"You thought he would stop looking for me?"

"Of course not, but he is angry and I do not want you hurt or Spensor and, and…" Tears gathered in her eyes and she was not even sure why.

"Oh, Betsy." Betsy focused as Angella put her hands on either side of her face and forced Betsy to look at her. "Betsy, you are in love with Edward. It is more than a childish hope or dream. You are, aren't you—really, truly in love?"

"Oh my." She swallowed and sighed. "I am, aren't I—hopelessly in love with your brother?" As Angella released her, she grabbed her friend's hands. "Angella, what will I do? He'll go away again and he'll never see me as a proper wife for him."

"Betsy, I have a feeling about this, so don't despair." Angella pursed her lips. "Let's invite him to the ball. A bit late, to be sure, but time enough."

"But you…and Spensor?"

"Will make him see the truth."

"Oh, Angella, we can't!" Betsy heard her wail and winced.

"Why ever not?"

"I have no notion where he resides. I've bungled everything—again!"

Angella's eyes glittered with purpose. "No, no, you haven't. We serve a God in the business of doing the impossible. I'll tell you what we're going to do."

Betsy sat forward. "What do you propose?"

"We pray and trust in the only one who can work it all out."

Betsy felt the air leave her lungs. "Yes, we shall pray."

"Now." Angella stared at her as though willing her to believe. "Trust me, Betsy. If God can work a miracle for your cousin and me, He can work things out for you and Edward."

Hope sprang up inside. Just maybe… The girls clasped hands and bowed their heads. "Lord Jesus…"

Later he realized she had done it to him again. By the time he alerted Lady Carrington, got them safely to their carriage and on the way home, the subject of Angella melted into the background.

As he swung into his mentor's book room, Edward repressed his frustration with difficultly. Other than his bedchambers, it was the room in which he could be most comfortable and think. He more slammed rather than tossed his gloves on a nearby stand as he sank into a cushioned Georgian-style chair in green and rust by the hearth that had long been cleaned out of ashes and replaced with a bouquet of spring flowers. The scent made him think of Betsy and his ire with her grew.

Yet how could he be wroth with her? Mayhap she really was not feeling well. Guilt mingled with his frustration and anger, more at himself than at her. How long had he been in London already and no closer to finding his sister? He groaned.

"My friend," sounded a deep voice close by, "what ails you this afternoon?"

Edward started, not realizing Reverend Jeremiah worked at the desk in the corner. He waited as the ponderous minister settled in the matching chair opposite his with a grace that belied his bulk. "I take it you did not find the lady this afternoon?"

"Actually, I did." Edward explained about the wrong house, the library and his frustration.

As he spoke, sometimes rather heatedly, the minister nodded. At times, the slightest of smiles played on his lips. "You believe Betsy is keeping you from your sister." It was not a question.

"Assuredly." Edward sat forward. "Do you not see?"

"Hmm." His mentor stroked his cheek with a long finger. "Do you? Son, if you truly wished to see to your sister, why spend so much time chasing after the young Miss Carrington?" He held up a hand to stop Edward's protestations. "I know you care about your sister, and you, rightly, have concerns. I also think your anger in her case is misplaced. That said…" He paused before continuing. "I believe the real problem is one of the heart."

"What!" Something curled into a knot inside. "Of what do you refer?"

His mentor's gaze discomfited him. "I believe your heart to be engaged. Did I not say Miss Carrington held the key to your sister? The problem is your heart."

"That cannot be. Cannot happen. India. My mission." Edward knew he babbled.

"There are other ways of finding Lucashire's whereabouts. You chose one. Why? When you answer that…" The minister left the implications for Edward to figure out.

The truth slowly dawned and he slumped. Had he not admitted he could not get her out of his thoughts? Yet, somehow, he'd kept himself from fully seeing Betsy as more than a dream. "I cannot be in—in love with Betsy." He all but whispered the last.

"Why ever not? She sounds like just the sort of woman who understands your calling. We touched on this subject before."

"I know, but how can I expect her to go to India, leaving behind all she's ever known. For what…? I have little enough to offer. How can I ask her? She is a lady."

"Of considerable sense, sounds to me." This time the minister patted Edward's knee. "How do you know how she will respond if you do not ask? Never knew you to be a coward, Edward."

"I am not…" Mayhap he was where she was concerned. "Do you really believe she would take kindly to my suit?"

"Ask her, son. Ask." With that his mentor got slowly to his feet. "As I said before, I do believe once you figure out what to do about young Miss Carrington, the problem with your sister will also untangle itself." Going to his desk, he returned with a card that he thrust into Edward's hands. "Here. It is an invitation to a ball at Alistair House. You might find some of your answers there." He left Edward staring down at the engraved invitation and wondering just how much his mentor knew about the whole situation. Alistair? Wasn't that the man he'd helped with the carriage? Edward gripped the invitation. Mayhap Alistair would be more helpful than he realized.

A certain something bubbled up inside when he murmured softly, "Betsy."

Now when he conjured her image it was not of a perfect, but unsubstantial young woman who worshiped at his feet. Instead, he knew Betsy was so much more, a real woman of substance, character and strength who was willing to protect his sister, yes, he realized it, even against himself. His cheek twitched as he thought back to his hopes and dreams. He groaned again at his proposal. It was less than honorable. Truly, Christian duty? How starched-up he must have sounded. Only a desperate woman would have accepted that proposal. No wonder he made Betsy cry. She cared for him, of that he was all but certain, but everything he did put her off.

He confronted his own behavior and found it wanting. Horror clutched his insides. Had he proposed in such a fashion to engender a refusal? *Oh, Lord, forgive me.*

He could only hope Betsy could forgive him as well, because he had an important question to ask. Edward gulped, his throat dry just considering speaking his heart to the vital, godly woman who was Miss Betsy Carrington.

Chapter 12

The evening was almost more than Edward could handle. It was all too much—the wealth of the jewels, the elegance of the clothing. He stared around the huge ballroom. Even the cost of the decorations would have kept him or another missionary for a long while on the field. He recognized men and women from his talks about his work in India. Many greeted him.

A tall peer with gray hair and almost black eyes spoke. "Reverend Denning, what brings you out tonight? Surely the entertainment does not include an appeal to our pocketbooks."

Edward's cheek twitched at the implications and he wished for nothing more than to run back out the door. Is this truly how many saw his efforts? He managed a civil reply. "I had an invitation as you did, my lord."

Sarcasm flashed in the man's eyes as he nodded

once more and took his leave. Others were more effusive in their consideration. Some wished to know about India itself or his work, and he tried to oblige those who asked. The positive comments almost—almost—wiped out the comments made by the sardonic peer when he first arrived.

Still and all, he tried to keep his sister in his sights... when his attention did not drift to Betsy, who looked elegant and beautiful. Several young bucks surrounded her, laughing and chatting until he all but clutched his hands together behind his back. At least two seemed to hold more than passing interest for her. He gritted his teeth.

As the evening progressed, he found himself not only worried his sister had been seduced by this opulent lifestyle, but also struggling with resentment at the style in which she lived.

Seeing her with the earl left him in no doubt that whatever had happened between them, Angella now fully accepted, relished even, her role in Lucashire's life. Sorrow more than anger, he realized, consumed him. But at the moment, there was nothing he could do but watch. Ladies and gentlemen smiled and nodded. He scarcely heard. His ears roared. His head pounded, but it was from much more than his anger at his sister, sorrow at her situation or even from his resentment.

Why had Reverend Jeremiah sent him here? He did not fit in with the glitz and glitter. He felt deuced awkward. The crush kept him from his sister, who seemed here and there, always speaking to this person or that. Besides, he decided it would be better to stay out of his sister's reach until he came to some conclusion. How or when, Edward had no notion. Still, he found him-

self staying away from the one person who first drew
him back to England.

Lucashire was never far from her side and seemed all
solicitation. Edward held back the force of his tangled
emotions and tried to stay unbiased. Mayhap there was
an explanation. After all, surely the ton would not accept a dalliance at a social affair. If they knew…Betsy
said he did not know the truth. Reverend Jeremiah implied much the same, and Edward suspected his mentor knew more of the situation than he himself realized.
What was he missing? Meanwhile, he watched, listened
and did little to involve himself in the round of dancing, cards and conversation.

Betsy tried to keep an eye on Edward, but it appeared he already had connections in town. She felt
his gaze on her more than once, and a few times he got
close enough to converse before being once more drawn
away when someone asked about India. When Angella
was in sight, she watched Edward's eyes narrow and
she tensed. Surely, he would not make a scene, not tonight, not at Angella and Spensor's engagement ball.
As it happened in their infrequent interactions, Edward
was halted or drawn away. She did not care for it on
her behalf, but she breathed relief when the interest in
India kept him from approaching Angella.

Betsy had to admit the man was all that was fashionable in a finely tailored black jacket, contrasting waistcoat, pantaloons and low-heeled shoes.

It discomfited her when Baron Fritton escorted her
onto the dance floor and stuttered his interest until his
manner irritated her to distraction. The marquis's manner suited her little better. He was not used to rejec-

tion and pulled her out into the garden to talk some sense into her. He was well situated, he told her, and could offer her a place in society. His insistence only forced her to bite her lip as she tried firmly, yet politely enough, to calm his ardor. All she wanted to do was be with Edward and, she admitted, to ensure he did not make a cake of himself.

It surprised Betsy that neither Angella nor the earl recognized Edward. After all, he was Angella's brother. Still and all, the room was large and filled with people, and she had not seen him for years. Edward's features had sharpened over the years and his body had grown lean and hard. To her, Edward was everything a man should be and her heartbeat quickened as once more she caught his eye. She smiled. He only seemed stunned.

Sometime later Betsy found Angella beside her. "Oh, Angella, congratulations," she told her friend, giving her a quick hug. "I hope tonight is all that is wonderful for you."

Betsy followed Angella's gaze toward Spensor. "God is blessing me with my heart's desire. It is all a dream, a wonderful dream."

"You deserve it. Enjoy to the fullest."

Angella nodded toward Edward, who was mostly hidden behind a portly gentleman and his equally proportioned spouse. "You seem to have made a conquest in the serious gentleman."

Betsy blushed, not sure how to go on. She grimaced when Angella continued. "He seems to hold me in low esteem, though. When he glances my way, he seems so angry." Angella paused. "He seems familiar somehow, but I never can get close enough to get a good look at him. You know him, I take it."

Betsy cleared her throat, frantically wondering what to say. "Uh, he is a clergyman. He spoke at the mission."

"I see." From the confusion on her face, it appeared that Angella still had questions.

Betsy took her arm and steered her back to Spensor. "I'm sure you'll meet him before the night is over."

"I'm sure you are correct…and yet…"

Betsy sighed with relief as Spensor escorted Angella away toward another couple.

The affair was a sad crush. Betsy didn't care. Trying to keep Edward in sight and away from Angella was exhausting. At one point she determined to pull him aside to see what he planned to do, but her mother intervened to ask for her help.

She kept an eye on Angella, as well. As the hours crawled by, Angella's shoulders sagged. Everyone but Edward made it a point to stop and wish Angella and Lucashire their best. Even her friend's smile drooped and Betsy wondered if Angella's lips stuck to her teeth.

It was nearly dawn before the last of the guests made their way to the door. Still Edward stayed on. Betsy sensed an explosion in the making and prayed.

She also savored Edward's touch on her hand, the look in his gaze that made the room feel overly warm and the request he made to see her later. Could there possibly be something more in his request?

Edward found it more and more difficult not to confront his sister. However, to his surprise, the event provided a perfect chance to speak of his work in India, from those who had already heard him speak and others who showed interest. He also seemed unable to stay away from Betsy, who glowed in her white gown with silver trim. He felt as though he walked on water whenever Betsy smiled at him and offered her hand. Edward could not let her go. "I…I need to speak with you," he managed to stutter. "Do…do you think you might make time for me?"

Betsy blushed. "Why, yes, I think I might. Tomorrow, no, this afternoon, then."

Like any dandy, Edward held and kissed her hand until Betsy herself tugged it from his grasp with a giggle. Embarrassed at his ninnyhammered behavior, Edward watched her go.

Much later, he turned and found himself face-to-face with Angella and the earl.

For all his plans to confront his sister, he now gulped, wondering how to go on. He had never considered that the earl would be so large or so overwhelming. His own offenses of anger and resentment made him hesitate. Somehow, glancing over toward where Betsy spoke to a short, round woman in a puce gown defused the fire inside. From all he'd seen during the long night, his sister was liked, respected and accepted. That certainly did not "fit" the image he'd built up in his mind.

It rather surprised him Angella had not discerned the truth of his identity. Mayhap it was because he'd made sure never to allow her to get too close or to get a good view of him. Besides, she wasn't expecting him at the event and her attention was probably on a hundred other things. She did look beautiful in a gown with roses embroidered around the modest neckline, waist and above the hem. She dressed as their mother would have desired, but never was able due to their meager income.

Though a slight smile touched the corners of the

earl's mouth, there was a question in his eyes. "I hope you enjoyed the evening, Mr....?"

"Reverend," he supplied. A muscle twitched in Edward's cheek. He was unused to subterfuge, but he was not certain he wanted to reveal himself yet. "It was most enlightening. I fear I am unused to such…uh, splendor." He could not completely disguise the resentment evident in his tone, which he never realized he held. Such feelings were lowering in the extreme.

His sister, Angella, smiled at him, her eyes twinkling mischievously in the way that used to both irritate and endear her to him. Now it raised his ire. How dare she act with such ingenuousness! Unless…unless… He closed his eyes momentarily against the questions clamoring for answers.

He watched Angella glance toward Lucashire for direction. Obviously she sensed something amiss with him. She always was quick-witted. "I say, Reverend," demanded the earl, "just what is it you want?"

Edward blinked. For one who had prided himself on his reliance on God, he found himself confused in the whirl of his emotions, emotions having nothing to do with the peace he had in his Heavenly Father. Peace! It seemed an age since he had known peace.

Was this, then, how it began? First the small sin, then the next, the next. How had it been for Angella? There was no hope now of coming out of this with his dignity intact.

"Angella." His familiarity brought a protest to the earl's lips, his arm surrounded her waist protectively. "Reverend, I say, do you have a problem?"

"No, yes. Listen…" Nothing came out. Fear glinted

on the face of his sister. Of a certain they thought him completely daft. Well, no wonder.

The Earl and Countess of Alistair walked by, hand in hand. "It was lovely, my dear." She kissed Angella's cheek. "I wish you both great happiness." Lord Alistair shook Lucashire's hand. He noticed Edward and nodded. "Thanks again for your assistance. Nice seeing you here tonight."

Edward stared after the couple as they made their way up the wide staircase. Servants bustled about them in the ballroom cleaning and straightening. In a couple of hours the room would show no evidence of having been swarmed with people.

Angella yawned behind her hand. Lines of exhaustion settled under her heavy lids. He knew the earl wished him gone, but was too much the gentleman to ask him to leave.

Angella leaned against the earl as she hid a yawn behind her gloved hand. The earl stepped forward. "Reverend, if you have business with me, fine, but I wish to send Miss Denning to her bed."

"Why, so you might join her later?"

The words ground out of Edward, surprising him as much as they infuriated the earl. He was not even sure he believed his own preconceived notions any longer. With everything in him, he wished to recall his accusation.

Angella gasped. Her eyes filled with tears.

The earl clenched his fists. "And just what does that mean? I think you have quite outstayed your welcome… Reverend. If you *are* a minister of the gospel."

Edward straightened. Everything he'd heard from the vicar and Lady Margaret rang in his mind. Rising in indignation to the threat, Edward straightened. "Fine gentleman you, taking an innocent young woman and seducing her to your bed without benefit of the wedding lines. I suppose you thought her not good enough for the likes of the Earl of Lucashire."

"And you." He turned his rage onto his sister. "How could you live with this libertine as though he were your husband? How could…" Edward could go no further. To his shame, tears coursed down his cheeks.

"Angella, how could you?"

"Are you mazed, sir?" Angella stared at him, puzzled. "Spensor has not shamed me in any way. We are even now planning our nuptials. Tonight we celebrated our engagement. Did you not know? Who told you differently? Surely you don't believe he would parade some doxy among the ton as his ward. It isn't done. I would never—"

The earl stepped between Angella and Edward. "How dare you accuse Miss Denning of such a disgraceful thing!"

In desperation, Edward cried, "But Lady Ainsworth saw you…" he lowered his voice "…in his chambers late one night."

Angella's face whitened. The earl, his lips tight with repressed anger, grabbed the man's arm. "I think you have some explaining to do, Reverend. I want an explanation, and I want it now. Just why does any of this concern you?"

Desperation stiffened Edward's shoulders. "Because I am Edward Denning, Angella's brother…and her legal guardian."

Angella gasped. Releasing Edward, the earl caught her as she fainted.

Edward felt as though his heart stopped until Angella slowly opened her eyes. She lay on a sofa with curved whorled feet, though Edward had no idea why he noticed that detail. Around the formal drawing room candles sputtered their last in the wall sconces. Only the candles in the tall shiny brass candelabrum on the small end table next to the sofa held tall, new candles that cast a golden shadow over the occupants. Though streaks of light at the edges of the heavy curtains proclaimed a new day, no one had yet bothered to pull open the drapes to welcome it.

The earl anxiously hovered over Edward's sister. "Angella, darling. Are you all right?"

Edward returned her stare as she studied him.

"Are you truly Edward, my brother?" Reluctantly, the earl permitted him to approach.

"I am. Angella. I am sorry, I thought… I don't understand, I mean." He felt unsure of himself.

"I thought you'd never come," whispered his sister, swallowing with difficulty. "I began to think you weren't coming back."

Edward clasped his hands behind his back, his heart sick. "I was pretty caught up in my work, I fear. I should have returned long since."

"Carey needed you?"

Though his sister gave him an out, Edward refused to take refuge in the easy admission. "There is always work to be done, Angella, but I have no excuse for not seeing to my family. Even Carey agreed I needed a break."

"You got my letter."

"Yes, and I returned as soon as possible."

"Why the subterfuge?" The earl's voice was hard. "You abused our hospitality."

"I know." Misery sat like a brick inside. There were questions still, but there was no gainsaying he had wrongly accused his sister. In so doing, he had made an absolute and complete cake of himself.

"As if your sister has not been through enough without having you denounce her without more proof than that of a vindictive woman."

"She was your fiancée," Edward said defensively. "She made some pretty damaging accusations. With what I'd already heard from the vicar who took Father's place, what was I to believe?"

Angella sighed. "I don't know, Edward, but coming here tonight as you did, then treating me all night as though I had some loathsome disease. You were never one to evade the truth of a matter before, why now?"

"Because I wanted to know the truth. Lady Ainsworth said she found you in the earl's chambers late one night."

"'Tis true," Angella began, stuttered when Edward's face paled and he sucked in a deep, shuddering breath. "Edward, listen. It wasn't as it seems."

Lucashire faced down the missionary. "Yes, your sister was with me. You wish for the truth. You shall hear it. The whole of it." Pointing to a nearby chair, he commanded, "Sit down, Reverend Denning."

Edward, frowning, did as he was told, his eyes on the cold face of the earl. He saw that face soften as the earl sat on the edge of the couch and took Angella's trembling hand in his. Lucashire's visage hardened again, as he once more speared Edward in his penetrating gaze.

"The good people of Little Cambrage were persuaded

your sister was not only deliberately trying to seduce the new vicar, who I might add, is the devil's own."

Edward swallowed with some difficulty. Was not that what the elderly woman had told him? Why had he not listened? "That's ridiculous."

"Of course it is." The earl actually snorted his disgust. "It was a hum. Reverend Carter wanted Angella for himself and when she soundly refused him, he had her driven out of the village with nothing but what she stood up in. He has now, I might add, been replaced.

"Had I not come along then, your sister would now probably be dead…or worse. When I arrived, the village bullies were trying to stone her."

Again Edward gasped. His hands clutched the arms of the chair. "How could they do such a thing?"

The earl's face softened as he continued. "Yes, I became her protector, her guardian, as—I might add—your mother wished."

Angella nodded, acknowledging this truth. Edward did not wish to hear more, but he knew he must.

"No, I did not influence her nearly as much as she influenced me." He smiled then, at Angella.

"Up until then I believed all Christians were sour-face hypocrites, claiming one thing, but doing another. Angella was anything but that. She was the most open, honest person I had ever met. And one who held her virtue highly. Her faith, too, was a very real and vital part of her. Her God worth serving.

"She was willing to die rather than obey me if it meant compromising her faith. She has quite the temper, I discovered."

A slight smile tickled Edward's lips, as well. "Aye,

I recall her temper, right well. Seems to be a family trait, I fear. But…"

Raising a hand, the earl continued. "I desired your sister, but I coveted her faith, as well."

Edward could not meet the earl's steady gaze. Too often, of late, he himself had been hypocritical. "I understand now about the vicar. I did not like him overmuch, either. I did not much credit what he said until I met up with Lady Ainsworth."

"Ah yes. My dear betrothed. She came to stake her claim because, once more, her brother was under the hatches. By then I wanted out of the farce. She and her brother could not wait." There was a cynical twist to the earl's lips. Angella closed her eyes, shuddered as though she recalled that night.

"Edward," Angella said, softly, "did you also become acquainted with Lady Margaret's younger brother, Herbert?"

"I did indeed. Seemed a rather slow fellow."

"Oh, Edward. Margaret decided that until I was discredited, Spensor would not marry her. She and Harry…" Angella could not go on.

Anger flashed in the earl's face, but his tenderness toward Angella was unmistakable. "She had the gall to instruct Herbert to go to your sister's room and attack her." Edward gasped, but the earl went on. "Thanks to her little cat, which was asleep on the bed, Angella was able to get away from him long enough to run to my study off my bedchambers.

"That is where Margaret found us. After I sent Margaret on her way, I tucked your sister in on the couch before the hearth while I went to my bedchambers. The next day I made provisions for Margaret and Harry and sent them out of our lives…I had hoped…permanently."

Edward bowed his head. The anger that had been a part of him for so long drained from him, leaving him confused and bewildered.

Silence. What was left to say? Even the hearth in the ballroom was cold and dead, having not yet been cleaned out for the day. A chill settled in the room, but it was nothing compared to the chill in Edward's heart.

He did not deserve Angella's regard and certainly not Betsy's. He was unworthy of his calling and yet it was all he had. Angella's future was assured as the beloved wife of the earl. He no longer doubted that. As for Betsy, how could he hold up his head after all the things he'd thought about her cousin and his own sister?

There was nothing to do but return to India as soon as possible. He was not sure how he accomplished it, but, not half an hour later, Edward found himself heading back to his mentor's home. He left Angella calling after him as he left the room, and he was sure he heard Betsy's voice as he drove away.

Chapter 13

After Edward drove off, Betsy hurried back into the drawing room. Under her breath she murmured, "Lord, please. I trusted You. Now what?"

Angella, still sitting on the sofa with Spensor beside her holding her hand, asked, "Did you speak with him?"

Betsy dropped into a nearby chair. "No. He drove off and would not acknowledge me." She paused. "I glimpsed his face. Oh, Angella, he looked absolutely broken. Whatever happened here? I only caught the end when he rushed away."

"You were right, Betsy. He….he made accusations."

"Oh dear."

"He was horrified when they slipped from his mouth and more so when he learned the truth."

Betsy wiped a tear from her eye that matched the one running down Angella's face as her friend sighed.

"Poor Edward. What he must have been going through, blaming himself for leaving me behind."

Lucashire straightened. "Poor Edward. My dear, what he thought…"

Angella patted his hand. "I know, but he was too angry and worried to think clearly." She glanced over at Betsy. "Especially since his mind has been on more than my situation."

Betsy felt color warm her cheeks. "He asked to see me later this afternoon, but…I'm afraid…now. You did not see his face. He was humiliated and hurting." She put her fears into words. "What if he doesn't return?"

"Betsy, we must find him." Angella turned to the earl. "What if, now that he knows I am all right, he leaves….for good. Spensor, I could not bear it if he left." From his response, Betsy knew her cousin caught the pain in Angella's voice.

"I am sorry." Betsy bit her lip. "But I have no idea where he resides."

"I have an idea." With that the earl got up and pulled the bell cord. When Davis answered, the earl said, "Please bring last night's invitations that were handed in."

Not long thereafter, the three thumbed through the engraved parchments. "Here. Yes." The earl held up an invitation. "I think your brother came on another's invitation."

Angella read the name and wrinkled her forehead in thought. Excitement danced in her eyes. "Yes. Yes. I recall now. That was Edward's mentor long past and a firm supporter of his ministry. If he is any place in London, that's where."

Betsy got to her feet. "Come, we have to find Edward."

Her cousin held up a hand. "I'll call for the curricle to be brought round. Meanwhile, my dear Angella and cousin, why not change your clothing into something more appropriate?"

The girls stared down at their formal gowns. Betsy grabbed Angella's hand. "Come on. Let's hurry."

Shame traveled with Edward. Betsy had been wise to keep him from seeing his sister. She was one wise, caring woman. Too bad he'd never discover if she would have accepted his heart.

He planned to go right up to his room and start packing, even knowing it would take time to find a ship to take him back to India. He fingered one of his father's books. Mayhap if he pawned them, he could get enough for the voyage.

However, his mentor caught him before he started up the stairs. "Hmm."

Edward started. "I am sorry. I did not see you standing there."

Reverend Jeremiah drew close, scrutinizing his face. "Something went horribly wrong." His gaze narrowed. "You did attend the ball, did you not?"

Edward turned to face Reverend Jeremiah. "I did and it was the biggest mistake of my life."

Taking his arm, his mentor and friend led him toward the library. Seeing no students within, he motioned Edward to a chair by the hearth, the same green-and-rust Georgian-style chair in which he'd sat not long past. It seemed like ages. This time there was no smile on the face of his mentor, who sat on the chair opposite. For a moment the man stared into the hearth, then up at Edward. "What happened last night?"

"This morning rather." Edward groaned. "You were right. Betsy was right. I should have confronted my anger and suspicions before confronting my sister."

Reverend Jeremiah stared at him in some consternation. "Are you saying you made accusations at the ball?"

"After most guests were gone. This morning."

A frown wrinkled the older man's forehead. "By then did you not realize the import of the evening?"

Edward shook his head and lowered it into his hands. "I did not listen to the tittle-tattle around me and tried to stay away from my sister and Lucashire. I simply watched, when I…"

"Wasn't occupied with the young woman who has captured your heart." This time a slight smile drew up the corners of the man's lips.

Raising his head, Edward took note and again shook his head. "I had no notion the affair was an engagement celebration until after…" he continued to explain.

His mentor sat back. "Oh, Edward. I hoped you would realize the folly of your suspicions. Now what do you propose to do?"

"What else to do? Angella is well situated. I cannot expect her or the earl or Betsy to ever forgive me. I will leave for India as soon as I can book passage." He sighed and slumped as though bearing the weight of the world—at least the weight of his actions and words. It was a heavy burden.

"So you let Betsy think you had intentions of asking for her hand, and now you will run out on her?"

Edward spread his hands. "I have nothing to offer

and now I have shamed myself before them with my rackety accusations."

Edward stared at his mentor. His hands clasped together. His heart a stone.

"So you are running away."

"No. Yes… I don't know anymore." Misery churned his stomach.

"You should know, Edward, that running away never solved any problem. You feel guilt over your actions and behavior. What will you do about that?"

"Repent, of course."

"You cannot do that here? Do you not think your sister, the earl and your young lady deserve an apology? Or is that too embarrassing for you?"

Edward squirmed. He did not like the picture of him painted by his mentor.

"Running away is not the answer, son. You'll only take this with you and it may well destroy your ministry. You need to confront the issue…and that starts with a time with the God who created you, loves you and understands us even when we do not understand ourselves."

As Edward nodded, Reverend Jeremiah leaned forward. "Shall we pray now?"

Edward merely nodded. The session that followed cleansed him and set him free as he had not felt free since visiting with the vicar. "Thank you, Jesus, for Your forgiveness when we come to You." When he raised his head, he smiled. "It is gone."

"Yes, I see that. Now what will you do?"

Edward stood. "If I can use your rig again, I have an important errand to attend at Alistair House, correct? That is where they are staying."

"It is."

"You knew."

His mentor merely smiled. "Go now."

Edward pulled on his gloves as he headed out the door. Suddenly he could not wait to see his sister… and Betsy.

By the time the young women arrayed themselves in walking dresses, Lucashire had the lightweight curricle out front. He quickly handed Angella and Betsy into the conveyance, where they squeezed together as he hopped on board and took up the reins.

At his signal, the perfectly matched bays with their shiny red coats and black manes and tails pulled on the traces. A moment later, they shifted into a trot and stretched out as Lucashire gave them rein. They were fresh and eager and the earl held them in a bit to keep control, while allowing them freedom to move as quickly as the road and traffic conditions allowed.

Betsy held on to Angella's cold hands. They exchanged glances and each read the concern on the face of the other. "We must find him." Angella spoke in Betsy's ear, who nodded her agreement.

There was little to say, but Betsy closed her eyes and tried to focus on prayer. Her disordered heart clouded her mind and she choked out a "Help us, Jesus" request. She felt the squeeze on her hand and knew Angella echoed her concern.

Regrets at how she had handled her contact with Edward sat heavy upon her. Yet, for all that, he had asked to speak with her…. Something about the expression in his eyes had given her hope. But now… Now she felt disaster crashing about her and suspected Angella felt much the same.

She sighed with relief when they reached their destination. An elderly servant showed them into the library, where her cousin stepped forward to greet the corpulent man rising to his feet. After their greeting, he asked, "What brings you here?"

"Edward," started Angella, "my brother—"

"Reverend Denning," added Betsy.

The earl finished, "He resides here, does he not?"

"He does."

Angella stepped forward. "We must speak with him straightaway."

Betsy thought she witnessed the hint of a smile on the man's lips. "To what purpose?"

For a moment no one spoke. The next all three spoke at once until the minister raised a hand. "One at a time, please."

Lucashire straightened. "I fear there has been a great misunderstanding and Edward rushed away before things could be resolved."

Angella said, "I fear he might do something rash."

Betsy heard the tremble in her tone. "Please, might we speak with him?"

For a long moment, the minister surveyed them. "He is not here."

"No!" Angella clasped her hands. "Surely he could not have left for India so soon."

Betsy gulped. "Please, Reverend."

"We spoke and yes, he had every intention of returning to his ministry, but right now..." he paused "...he is headed to Alistair House to set things right. I suggest—"

Betsy interrupted, "We head back there immediately." Realizing her lack of manners, she flushed. Though from the twinkle in the man's eyes, she knew he understood.

Not long thereafter, the now not-so-fresh horses headed back to Alistair House. Betsy cried, "What if we miss him?"

"We won't." Her cousin stood as he directed the horses. "I know a few shortcuts."

He did and they weren't through the nicest parts of town, but it was not long before he handed them out of the curricle and escorted them back into the house.

"Davies, has Reverend Denning arrived?"

The butler acknowledged the earl. "I thought you'd return, so I put him in the east parlor."

Angella all but bounced up and down. Betsy sighed with relief. Her cousin held out his arms and escorted them to Edward.

Hearing the door open, Edward turned. His stomach knotted in dread at seeing the three enter. He must get this over with before he lost his courage completely. As the three drew close, he opened his mouth, but Lucashire forestalled him. "Let us sit." They did, staring at one another awkwardly.

Edward, unable to stay seated, rose. He gulped, paced. "I tender my apologies for running away. I am deeply shamed by my behavior."

Angella reached for his arm as he passed by, but missed. "Oh, Edward. You do not need—"

"Yes, sis, I do." He gathered his thoughts. "There are those who do what they do for the glory and honor of men. There are others who do not even realize they are betraying their faith, their personal values and standards until it is done. At some time or other we're all hypocrites, doing or being something that we do not feel inside. Truth is, without a personal relationship with Jesus Christ, we can be little else."

He paused, bit his lip as he glanced toward Lucashire and away. "I never thought to feel this way. I've never known such anger as I've felt for you these past weeks. To my shame, I must confess I nurtured it, let it consume me. Even while I spoke of my great love for the Indian natives, I let my feelings blot out rational thought. My relationship with my Heavenly Father suffered, as well." He sighed deeply.

"For all that, for the distress I have caused you, I am truly repentant." He tried to smile. Failed.

"I tried to run. Afraid my mentor had something to say about that." Edward shook his head, taking in his audience, who listened, scarcely breathing. "I can wallow in my own misery, but I know God forgives. He has forgiven me…will you, can you forgive me, as well?" His voice broke as he knelt before his sister where she sat next to the earl on the sofa.

Tears started in Angella's eyes and coursed down her cheeks.

"Angella?"

"I…do…forgive you, Edward. I love you."

"You have my forgiveness, too, Edward." Lucashire held out his hand. Edward gripped his firmly. As he rose to his feet, Angella wept against Lucashire's shoulder. The look on the man's face revealed more than anything else the tenderness he felt for Angella. How could Edward not have realized during the ball when he thought he'd been observing with such objectivity?

As she gathered her composure, Angella sniffed, wiped her eyes on the linen square the earl handed her and asked, "Edward, you will stay until after the wedding, will you not? I do so wish you to give me away."

"You want me to stay?" Edward gulped. He really would like to be here to see his sister married.

"We would. Sponsor?" Angella turned to her betrothed, her face a question. Lucashire glanced from her to Edward. "You must stay, Edward. It will please your sister…and myself."

"Then I shall stay. Thank you." He hardly knew how to deal with the enormity of their forgiveness. He'd returned to see to his sister. She had found her feet right and tight. He could return to India with a clear conscience—and as soon as possible.

The voice inside asked, "What about Betsy?"

Yes, he needed to make amends there, as well. Angella and the earl seemed to be of the same mind. The earl assisted Angella to her feet as he nodded toward his cousin. "Edward, I think you wanted to speak with Betsy." With that, they left the room, leaving him facing the one woman who took away his breath and tied his tongue.

Edward beheld the doubt on Betsy's face. "Edward?" Uncertainty sounded in her tone. Edward picked up on it and color suffused his cheeks as she continued. "If you do not wish to speak with me, it—it is all right."

"No. I mean yes. I do wish to speak with you. Must speak with you," he babbled and flushed in turn.

Betsy tugged his arm. "Edward, calm down. I will not ring a peal over you for running away. I am sorry I got in the way of you seeing your sister. I should not…"

This time, Edward sucked in a breath. "Yes. Yes you

should have. You did what you needed to do to protect my sister and…" a crooked smile formed on his lips as he continued "…your cousin. I thank you for almost saving me from myself."

"Almost?"

"I did rather make a cake of myself earlier this morning in the drawing room." He shook his head. "I am so sorry, Betsy. More than I can convey."

She nodded. "And I accept. I am glad you shall remain for the wedding. I take it you will then return to India." She blinked back tears as she faltered on the words.

His heart cried out. *Oh, Betsy.* The thought of leaving her behind already felt devastating.

As though coming to a decision, Edward held out his hand. When she placed hers in his, he drew her to her feet. Her hands felt cold in his. "You would miss me?"

Confusion brought a delightful blush to her cheeks at the intensity of his gaze. She bit her lip, pulled her hands free and tugged at her sleeve, all nervous gestures Edward now recognized. "Very much so."

Edward tucked her hand in his elbow and led her to the large patterned sofa by the hearth filled with flowers. Their fragrance overpowered the senses. He felt Betsy tremble. He did not wish to frighten her, but she had to know the truth of his life.

"Betsy, my life is not easy. I have little, hours are long. Amenities are few as is contact with other British citizens." He continued. "The people of India are colorful and caring. But there are so many needs and there is such darkness. Conversions are few and difficult because following Christ doesn't just mean a change of religions, but often a death sentence from a convert's own family."

Betsy gasped and wiped tears starting in her eyes. "How sad. They need so much. Oh, Edward, I envy you the opportunity."

He sat up as hope settled in his eyes. "Truly. Envy?"

"La." Betsy frowned. "I'll miss wrangling with you."

"Betsy." Edward took her hand. "Is there someone else? Does anyone hold your heart? I saw…"

Betsy shook her head. "Afraid the marquis tried to press his suit, but no…there is no one… As for Fritton, he is more like a brother than a suitor, though he wishes differently."

Edward did not wait for her to finish. "I have no right to ask. I have no title or expectations. My work is far from England and your mother. But…but…you have captured my heart. Would you, possibly, at least consider marriage to a missionary—me? I know—"

"Yes." Betsy's gaze caught and held his own.

"What?" Her answer stunned him. Mayhap she did not understand.

A tiny smile lifted Betsy's lips. "I said, yes, Edward. Yes, I will marry you."

For a moment, Edward stared at her. Then with aching gentleness, he took her in his arms, leaned over and pressed his lips to hers.

Epilogue

The Earl of Alistair, dressed to the nines in a black jacket, entered the room, filled with Georgian furnishings, in which Betsy and Angella waited. Angella turned so quickly, Betsy grabbed her arm to steady her. Angella's gown eddied around her silver slippered feet. Vertical silver threads made the white gown sparkle. The long, tight sleeves ended in a delicate ruffle echoed along the hem line. The neckline ended in a modest V that showed off the Lucashire emerald necklace.

Betsy surveyed her own gown of antique white with a square neckline and short puffed sleeves that set off her shoulders. The bodice sparkled with pearl insets.

She'd never had a gown so fine and could not wait to stand before Edward at the altar. She smiled. Had it been but two weeks ago she and Edward announced their engagement? Angella would hear of nothing less than a double wedding, causing everything to be sixes and sevens in preparation.

Her concern for her mother turned into a surprise when her mother confided she had little reason to stay in England. If the couple did not mind, she would like to travel with them to India, though she would stay with the other British citizens once they arrived. Lucashire, she said, would see to the estate.

To Edward's amazement and gratitude both Lucashire and Alistair agreed to send regular support. Through it all, Betsy walked in a fog, soaking up the love and attention Edward showered upon her. Even with her head muddled, things came together until, today, she would become Edward's wife. How far she'd come from the young girl who fell in love with him from a painting.

Angella clasped her hands, whispering, "Soon you will, in truth, be my sister."

Bowing, Alistair held out his arms. Angella's face lit with joy as she put her hand on his arm. Betsy's hand shook as she took his other arm. In two days' time she and Edward, along with her mother, would board a ship for India. No merchant ship this time. Lucashire made arrangements on the finest vessel sailing south and called it a gift from himself and Angella. Betsy swallowed the lump in her throat. God was indeed a God who was working even when she thought all was lost. Mayhap through it all she had finally learned, at least in a small way, to trust the Lord really did know best.

As the soft music sounded and the doors opened, she and Angella stepped forward to meet their bridegrooms.

* * * * *

REQUEST YOUR FREE BOOKS!

2 FREE INSPIRATIONAL NOVELS
PLUS 2
FREE
MYSTERY GIFTS

Love Inspired

YES! Please send me 2 FREE Love Inspired® novels and my 2 FREE mystery gifts (gifts are worth about $10). After receiving them, if I don't wish to receive any more books, I can return the shipping statement marked "cancel." If I don't cancel, I will receive 6 brand-new novels every month and be billed just $4.74 per book in the U.S. or $5.24 per book in Canada. That's a savings of at least 21% off the cover price. It's quite a bargain! Shipping and handling is just 50¢ per book in the U.S. and 75¢ per book in Canada.* I understand that accepting the 2 free books and gifts places me under no obligation to buy anything. I can always return a shipment and cancel at any time. Even if I never buy another book, the two free books and gifts are mine to keep forever.

105/305 IDN F49N

Name _____ (PLEASE PRINT) _____

Address _____ Apt. #

City _____ State/Prov. _____ Zip/Postal Code

Signature (if under 18, a parent or guardian must sign)

Mail to the Harlequin® Reader Service:
IN U.S.A.: P.O. Box 1867, Buffalo, NY 14240-1867
IN CANADA: P.O. Box 609, Fort Erie, Ontario L2A 5X3

**Are you a subscriber to Love Inspired books
and want to receive the larger-print edition?
Call 1-800-873-8635 or visit www.ReaderService.com.**

* Terms and prices subject to change without notice. Prices do not include applicable taxes. Sales tax applicable in N.Y. Canadian residents will be charged applicable taxes. Offer not valid in Quebec. This offer is limited to one order per household. Not valid for current subscribers to Love Inspired books. All orders subject to credit approval. Credit or debit balances in a customer's account(s) may be offset by any other outstanding balance owed by or to the customer. Please allow 4 to 6 weeks for delivery. Offer available while quantities last.

Your Privacy—The Harlequin® Reader Service is committed to protecting your privacy. Our Privacy Policy is available online at www.ReaderService.com or upon request from the Harlequin Reader Service.
We make a portion of our mailing list available to reputable third parties that offer products we believe may interest you. If you prefer that we not exchange your name with third parties, or if you wish to clarify or modify your communication preferences, please visit us at www.ReaderService.com/consumerchoice or write to us at Harlequin Reader Service Preference Service, P.O. Box 9062, Buffalo, NY 14269. Include your complete name and address.

LIDIR13R

REQUEST YOUR FREE BOOKS!

2 FREE INSPIRATIONAL NOVELS
PLUS 2
FREE
MYSTERY GIFTS

Love Inspired.
HISTORICAL
INSPIRATIONAL HISTORICAL ROMANCE

LIHDIR13R